THE LAST WARNING

Detective-Superintendent Budd is a busy man. In Thatchford on a minor investigation, calling on his old friend Superintendent Hawkins, he's asked to help with a murder mystery. One man has been stabbed, two of his business associates have been threatened. Then another murder takes place in a locked room with police guards outside . . . The case bristles with difficulties, but Budd sifts all the clues with his usual thoroughness, and exposes a dastardly plot.

GERALD VERNER

THE LAST WARNING

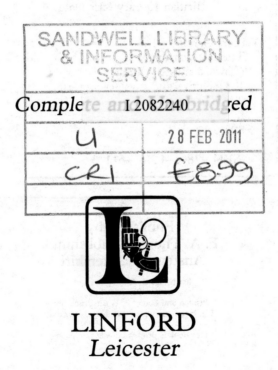

LINFORD
Leicester

First published in Great Britain

First Linford Edition
published 2011

British Library CIP Data

Verner, Gerald.
  The last warning. - -
  (Linford mystery library)
  1. Detective and mystery stories.
  2. Large type books.
  I. Title II. Series
  823.9'12–dc22

ISBN 978–1–44480–611–3

Published by
F. A. Thorpe (Publishing)
Anstey, Leicestershire

Set by Words & Graphics Ltd.
Anstey, Leicestershire
Printed and bound in Great Britain by
T. J. International Ltd., Padstow, Cornwall

This book is printed on acid-free paper

1

It was on the evening of Friday, the thirteenth of November, that Mr. Criller first saw the mark on his gate that marred the virgin whiteness of the paint-work.

Curiously enough he apparently attached no significance either to the roughly scrawled capital 'S' in red chalk or to the date. He was merely annoyed at this wilful desecration of his property, and curtly ordered his long-suffering housekeeper to see that it was removed at once.

He referred to it during dinner that evening, and Grace Hatton listened without interest, for she was used to his grumblings.

In the light from the four candles on the oval table his thin face looked even yellower than usual. He was a lean, complaining old man, with a lined face, a high, bald head, and his principal peculiarity was an excessive meanness.

The servants all hated him and even

Grace found him trying at times. But the servants had the advantage, for they could leave when they liked, whereas she was held by a bond more enduring than a contract.

She was a slim girl, with that pale prettiness that some men find attractive; a girl, who, when she smiled — which in that house was seldom — was really beautiful. She acted as a kind of unofficial secretary to the old man and, in return, was provided with food and shelter and a miscroscopic dress allowance, that amounted to less than the earnings of the kitchenmaid.

She called him 'uncle' at his own express wish, but the relationship had no basis in fact. Once, in a fit of bad temper, he had told her that she was the daughter of a former employee of his who had died, but when she had tried to question him further he had gruffly refused to discuss the matter.

She looked at him, now, as he sat hunched up in his high-backed chair, sipping his wine in silence, and wondered, as she had often wondered before, what had induced him to do what he had done for her. But she knew that it would be useless to ask. He looked very old and frail as he sat there, but she was aware that this was an illusion that he liked to cultivate. He was neither as old nor as weak as he appeared.

He raised his eyes from his plate and looked across at her.

'What time is that man coming in the morning?' he demanded in his harsh voice.

'Do you mean Mr. Brinn?' she asked.

'Of course I mean Brinn,' he snapped impatiently. 'There's only one man coming. Don't be a fool, girl!'

She was used to these querulous moods and ignored them.

'I'm not sure . . . ' she began.

'Get the letter,' he interrupted irritably. 'Get the letter!'

She got up obediently, and crossed the hall to the study.

It was a big, bare room with a huge desk and many filing cabinets. It looked more like an office than a room in a private house. Mr. Criller, although officially retired, still got through an enormous quantity of business. She found the letter in a folder on the desk, and carried it back to the dining room. The old man snatched it from her, growled something under his breath, and read it with a frown.

'He's coming at eleven-thirty,' she remarked, as she resumed her place at the table.

'I can read that for myself,' he snarled.

He laid the letter down beside his plate.

'I shall want that draft prospectus,' he went on. 'Have it ready for me by ten. I shall have time to go through it before Brinn arrives. Don't be late.'

He reached for the decanter and poured himself out another glass of port. He invariably had two, never more and never less.

'And while I remember it,' he continued, twisting the stem of the glass between his fingers. 'You'll behave yourself this time, you understand? I won't have any more trouble.'

The red crept into her cheeks.

'It was Mr. Brinn's fault, not mine,' she

said with a sudden flash of spirit. 'He tried to kiss me . . . '

'If he wants to kiss you, let him!' snarled the old man.

'I shall do nothing of the sort,' she retorted. 'Allowing your friends to make love to me is not one of my duties.'

'Your duty is to do as you're told,' growled Mr. Criller. 'Understand that. You're getting too high and mighty. You owe everything to me, and don't forget it.!'

He brought his fist down on the table to emphasise his words, and the wine splashed over the edge of his glass and formed a little pool on the polished table. His yellow face went a shade paler.

'Get a cloth,' he said huskily. 'Get a cloth and wipe that up. Go on, girl — be quick, d'you hear? It — it looks like blood . . . '

She stared at him in astonishment. He was cowering back in his chair, his rage gone, his eyes fixed on the little pool of spilt port as though it had been a poisonous snake. Picking up her napkin she came round to his side of the table and mopped up the wine with the square

5

of linen. He uttered a grunt of relief as she went back to her chair.

'I'm a fool,' he muttered, taking out his handkerchief and wiping his moist face. 'Getting old, that's what's the matter. That reminded me . . . ' He broke off abruptly, thrust the handkerchief back in his pocket and rose to his feet. 'I'm going to my room,' he growled. 'I shan't come down again.'

He went over to the door, opened it, and left the dining room.

She was glad to be left alone, but rather puzzled at the reason for his sudden retirement. Usually he spent several hours in his study after dinner, working, and four nights out of six she was kept busy taking notes from his dictation until after midnight.

But tonight something had upset him — some memory induced by the sight of that innocent pool of spilt port.

She went over to the big window and looked out into the darkness of the November night. She was still standing there when the housemaid came in to clear away.

'It's a nasty night, miss,' volunteered the girl. 'It's started to rain again.'

'Is it raining very heavily?' asked Grace.

The girl shook her head.

'No, just a bit of a drizzle,' she replied, and then curiously: 'You're not goin' out, are you, miss?'

Grace nodded.

'There are some letters to be posted,' she said.

'Ada'll take 'em, miss . . . ' began the girl, but Grace interrupted her.

'I'll take them,' she said.

She waited until the girl had finished clearing away and then, going up to her room, she exchanged her high-heeled shoes for a pair of brogues, wrapped a scarf round her head, and slipped on a raincoat.

It was half past nine when she left the house by the French window in the study and made her way down the tree-lined drive. She carried three letters in her hand, but they were not important, and merely served as an excuse for her going out. Mr. Criller always referred grandiloquently to the twisting path that ran up

7

from the gate to the front door as 'the drive,' but it was dignified by this name, being too narrow for any vehicle. It ended in a white-painted gate that gave on to a lane, and as Grace opened this a man who had been standing in the doubtful shelter of the hedge stepped forward.

'Is that you, Grace?' he asked in a low voice, and when she replied in the affirmative: 'How did you manage to get away from that old skinflint?'

She told him, and he whistled softly.

'Sounds as if the old devil had something on his conscience,' he commented. He took her arm and led her gently down the lane. 'How long are you going to put up with this impossible life?' he asked.

She made a weary gesture.

'Don't let's go into all that again, Jim,' she answered. 'I've told you there are reasons why I've got to stick it.'

Jim Longdon shrugged his shoulders.

'But you won't tell me what they are,' he retorted. 'I can't see any good reason why you . . . '

'And I can't offer you one,' she

interrupted. 'I wish I could tell you . . . There is a very good reason, but you'll have to take my word for it.'

Mr. Criller, who knew most things, knew nothing of her friendship with the good-looking young man who lived with his mother at Yule Lodge, the big white house at the top of the High Street. It was the one secret she had kept from him. The acquaintance had started eight months previously and had developed rapidly.

For one wild moment she thought of confiding her secret to the straight-backed young man by her side, and then reason asserted itself and she checked the words which rose to her lips.

They stood talking about nothing in particular for several minutes, and then, suddenly realising that time was passing, she turned reluctantly away.

'I must go back,' she said. 'I've been out longer now than I should have been.'

Jim Longdon would have liked to try to persuade her to stay, but he knew from experience that it would be no good. He walked with her to the white gate, where they said good night, and she almost ran up the path to the house.

The study windows were open, as she had left them. With a heavy heart she went in, shutting and fastening them behind her.

She was back in her prison, serving a sentence from which only death could release her.

★ ★ ★

The morning was bright and warm. The rain of the night before had stopped and the world lay bathed in yellow sunlight. From the window of her bedroom, Grace could see across miles of open country, for Mr. Criller's house was sited on a hill, and the loveliness of the view did something to lighten the trouble in her heart.

She turned away from the window at last with a little sigh of regret and made her way down the stairs. It was already nearly nine o'clock and she had a lot of work to do if she wanted to get the prospectus, which the old man had told her about, finished by ten.

She had a cup of tea and half a slice of toast for her breakfast and went into her little office, a tiny room adjoining the big study. Mr. Criller would be down punctually at nine-thirty.

She was busily typing when she heard his uncertain step pass the door and enter the dining room. It was ten minutes past ten before she had finished her task. She clipped the typewritten sheets neatly together and carried them into the study.

He was sitting at the big desk glowering at a letter which was spread on the blotting-pad in front of him. Grace laid the typed sheets silently on the desk. Without a word, he picked them up and read them swiftly but thoroughly.

She knew that he was looking for mistakes, and would be disappointed if he failed to find any.

'This is all right,' he remarked grudgingly, and laid the document aside. 'Now fetch your book. I've a lot of letters to dictate.'

She fetched her notebook and for the next hour he kept her busy, dictating rapidly without a pause.

'Do those at once,' he snapped when he had finished. 'I want them to catch the midday post.' She was turning to the door when he called her back. 'Where did you go last night?' he demanded curtly.

'I — I went out to post some letters,' She stammered slightly, for the question had been sudden and unexpected.

'You were gone a long time. I saw you go, and come back, from my window.' He glared at her suspiciously. 'Was that fellow Longdon about, eh?'

So he knew!

He saw the dismay in her face and his thin mouth hardened.

'I'll not have any philandering, understand that,' he said harshly. 'Oh, yes, I knew you were meeting him. It's got to stop, understand? You know why.'

She opened her lips to speak, but he silenced her with a gesture.

'I don't want to hear any excuses,' he rasped. 'Go and get on with your work, I'm busy.'

He sat for some time after she had gone, staring at the papers on his desk, the fingers of one bony hand playing with his lips. He was still sitting there, hunched up in his chair, when there came a tap on the door, and the maid entered to announced the arrival of his guest.

Mr. Franklin Brinn was a big, coarse-featured man, very red of face, with suspiciously black hair, and teeth whose evenness and whiteness owed nothing to nature. He affected a certain loudness of dress that matched his voice, for he spoke with a booming huskiness which he hoped would pass for good-fellowship.

''Mornin', Criller,' he greeted, as he swaggered into the room, and held out a huge hand.

The old man barely touched it with the tips of his fingers and indicated a chair.

'Sit down, Brinn,' he grunted. 'I've got the prospectus here for you.'

Franklin Brinn held up a protesting hand as he dropped heavily into the chair.

'My dear fellow, there's no hurry,' he said. 'What a man you are for busi-ness . . . '

'That's what you've come for, isn't it?' demanded Mr. Criller coldly.

'Yes, yes, but don't rush me before I've got my head inside the house,' answered the big man. 'There's plenty of time.'

The old man growled something below his breath and Brinn showed his teeth in a wide grin.

'You always were fond of rushing things,' he said. 'We might have cleared up a bit more over that bank business if you hadn't been in such a hurry . . .'

'We might also have got ten years!' retorted Criller. 'Remember that, Brinn! We probably would have done if you and Gottleib hadn't listened to me.'

'How is Gottleib?' asked Mr. Brinn, producing a silver case and selecting a cigar.

'He's all right, I suppose. I seldom see anything of him,' replied the old man. 'Now, let's get down to business.'

It was nearly lunch-time before they had finished arguing over the clauses in the prospectus, and when Mr. Criller finally folded the document and locked it away in one of the drawers in his desk Brinn gave an audible sigh of relief.

'Well, that's that,' he said. 'We ought to

clear up a packet over that.'

'Two hundred thousand,' snapped the other curtly.

'An' everythin' open an' above board,' commented Mr. Brinn with a chuckle. 'That's what I like about it. Nothin' crooked, eh? Honesty's the best policy in the long run.'

'Honesty's all right, if you can afford it,' grunted the old man.

'An' we can, eh?' grinned Brinn. 'That little business twenty years ago, eh? You an' me an' Gottleib scooped a nice packet. An' it's grown since. You must be worth a pretty penny, eh, Criller?'

'What I'm worth's my own business,' snapped Criller.

'I'll bet you're the richest of us all,' said Brinn. 'Still got that pretty girl, eh?'

'Yes, she's here,' said the old man, 'and you can leave her alone, Brinn. I'm not going to have her annoyed, understand?'

Brinn gave him a sly smile.

'Jealous?' he inquired. 'Bit sweet on her yourself, eh? You wicked old devil!'

'Don't talk nonsense,' snarled Mr. Criller. 'Grace is useful. When she's

15

annoyed it affects her work.' He turned his head rather pointedly towards the window. 'Lunch will be ready in half an hour,' he said. 'If you must smoke that cigar, go and smoke it in the garden.'

'I will,' said Brinn, and promptly availed himself of the invitation. He strolled across the lawn and down a side path that ended in a small summerhouse, and as he went he smoked contentedly . . .

Grace saw him go from the window of her tiny office and sighed with relief. She hated Franklin Brinn and his rough and clumsy attempts at love-making, and she had been dreading a meeting. Now she could take the letters into Mr. Criller while he was out of the way.

She tapped on the closed door of the study, but there was no reply, and, looking in, she saw that the big room was empty. Concluding that the old man had followed his friend into the garden, she laid the letters on his desk and went upstairs to her room.

She was washing her hands when the gong went for luncheon, and hurriedly drying them and tidying her hair she hurried down to the dining room.

Mr. Criller was standing by the window looking out, and he turned as she entered.

'Go and find Brinn,' he ordered curtly. 'He's in the garden somewhere. I hate being kept waiting for my meals.'

She had seen Brinn making for the little path that led to the summerhouse and turned her steps in that direction. The path passed through the centre of a thick belt of shrubbery, and the little rustic building was built on a raised brick dais at the end.

A bend in the path hid it from view until she was almost on it, and, as she rounded the corner, she saw the man she was seeking sitting at the round wooden table.

She called to him, but he did not look up, and at first she thought he had fallen asleep.

And then she saw . . .

There was blood on the floor and on the chair in which he sat. There was blood, too, on the front of the light waistcoat he was wearing . . . A spreading crimson patch from the centre of which protruded the black hilt of a knife . . .

She would never have cause to fear Franklin Brinn again.

He was dead!

2

Grace Hatton kept her head. She neither screamed nor fainted. For a moment she stood motionless, whitefaced and shaking, staring at the horrible thing in the chair. Then she turned and ran blindly back along the little path to the house.

As she crossed the lawn she saw Mr. Criller come out of the dining room windows and look towards her.

'What's the matter, girl?' he demanded as she stumbled breathlessly up to him. 'Where's Brinn?'

'He's . . . he's dead,' she panted, and he glared at her.

'What's that?' he snarled, gripping her arm with his lean fingers. 'Nonsense!'

'It's true,' she whispered. 'He's dead . . . in the little summerhouse . . . Let me go, you're hurting me . . . '

'You're lying!' His thin voice rose almost to a squeak. 'You're lying . . . '

She wrenched her arm free from his grip.

'If you don't believe me, go and look for yourself,' she said. 'He's dead. He's been stabbed . . . '

'Stabbed?' He raised a shaking hand to his mouth and the yellow of his face turned to grey. 'Who could have stabbed him?'

'Hadn't I better telephone for the police and a doctor?' she asked practically, but apparently he did not hear, for she had to repeat her question.

'Eh, what's that?' he snapped. 'No . . . no, not yet. I must see him first.'

With uncertain steps he walked to the path that led to the summerhouse. Grace hesitated a moment and then she followed him. He appeared to be quite unconscious of her presence, for he neither looked at her nor spoke as they followed the twisting path.

They reached the little building, and the old man stopped, staring at the slumped figure of Franklin Brinn. His lips moved and he muttered something below his breath, but the girl could not catch what he said. He made no attempt to go closer than the doorway, but stood peering at the body from the foot of the steps.

Presently he roused himself and turned a haggard face towards the girl.

'Go and telephone to the police,' he said huskily. 'Tell them to come up here at once . . . ' He swayed, and thinking he was going to fall she came to his side and offered a supporting arm. But he thrust her away.

'I'm all right . . . I'm all right,' he said testily. 'Don't waste time, girl. Get the police — get them quickly . . . '

She left him standing there and went back to the house.

The telephone stood on the big desk in the study. She lifted the receiver and was soon connected with the police station and pouring out her story into the interested ear of the sergeant in charge.

'I'll send along at once, miss,' he said. 'See that nothing is touched until the police get there.'

She hung up the receiver and returned to Mr. Criller. He was still standing where she had left him and he looked round at her approach.

'Are they coming?' he asked anxiously. 'How long will they be?'

She told him what the sergeant had said, and he seemed satisfied.

'Poor Brinn,' he muttered. 'Dead! It doesn't seem possible.'

He ascended the shallow steps and was entering the little house when she remembered what the sergeant had said about not touching anything, and warned him.

'I'm not going to touch him,' he snapped testily. He looked down at the obese figure, even coarser and uglier in death than it had been in life, and then he saw the roughly scrawled 'S' in red on the table-top and swung round towards the girl.

'Why didn't you tell me about that?' he demanded harshly. 'You never mentioned it. Why didn't you?'

His thin face was working and his eyes glared at her.

'What?' From where she stood at the bottom of the steps she could see nothing.

'This!' He motioned her to come

closer. 'See? The same mark that was on the gate.'

He pointed with a shaking finger at the table-top. Reaching his side, she looked down, and now she could see what was causing him so much agitation. On the plain wooden top of the little round garden table had been drawn a rough letter 'S' by a finger dipped in the dead man's blood.

'On the gate and on this table,' muttered the old man. 'What does it mean?' And then a hitherto sealed cell in his memory opened and he staggered back against the wall, his face so white that the girl thought he was going to faint. 'My God, it can't be,' he whispered huskily. 'It can't be! It's impossible. After all these years . . . '

'What's the matter?' she asked anxiously.

He recovered himself quickly.

'Nothing — nothing,' he answered, his voice almost inaudible. 'It was the shock . . . My heart . . . not as strong as it used to be . . . Help me back to the house.'

She took his arm, and leaning heavily on her, he stumbled back along the path to the house.

He was badly shaken — she could see — but there was something in his eyes that was more than horror at the tragedy that had taken place in his garden. There was fear — fear, not for what *had* happened, but for what might happen yet.

He stood for a moment, when they reached the dining room, staring at the window, his nervous fingers plucking at his lips, and then without a word he turned abruptly and almost staggered from the room.

She heard him go stumbling up the stairs to his room; heard the door slammed and the key turned in the lock. He had locked himself in from whatever it was he feared . . .

★   ★   ★

It was a small matter which brought that stout and sleepy-eyed man, Detective-Superintendent Budd, to Hertfordshire on that bright November morning. There

24

had been a robbery in a country house near Thatchford. It was an isolated case and the robber had been caught before he could make his getaway. He was a well-known 'ladder larcenist' named Whipper — a most appropriate name — and when the stout man heard that he was languishing in a cell he was interested.

He had been looking for Mr. Whipper for several months in connection with a case, in the mistaken hope, as it proved, that the little thief could supply him with some information.

Mr. Budd's journey, so far as the information he wanted, had been a waste of time, but while he was in the district he decided that he would drop in and see his friend, Superintendent Hawkins, at Thatchford.

Hawkins had been transferred from the Metropolitan Police at his own request a few years previously. In the old days — very far away they seemed now — Hawkins and Mr. Budd had walked a beat together as uniformed constables. Whenever the stout man had the opportunity, he liked to call on his old friend and chat over old times.

Hawkins greeted his friend with a smile of pleasure. He was a thinnish man, with the florid face and keenness of eye that comes from long hours spent in the open air.

'Well, this *is* a surprise,' he said as they shook hands. 'What's brought you this way, Budd?'

The stout superintendent explained, and Hawkins's eyes twinkled.

'That's the first bit of excitement we've had round here since Cobb's hayrick caught fire,' he said. 'Whipper was seen coming down a ladder at Mrs. Longdon's house. You must have passed it on the way here — big place with stone griffins on the gateposts?'

'I recollect it,' said Mr. Budd, nodding ponderously.

'The butler saw the man and held on to him while he got the police,' continued the local superintendent. 'He would have got away with quite a good bit of jewellery, which he swore we put in his pockets after his arrest. We don't get much excitement,' he added regretfully. 'It's a pretty quiet life.'

'I envy you,' remarked Mr. Budd. 'I could do with a bit of your peace and quietness.'

'Wouldn't suit you,' said Hawkins. 'You'd soon get sick of it. I do sometimes . . . '

He stopped as there came a tap at the door and a uniformed sergeant entered.

'Just had a message from Mr. Criller's house, Super,' he said, and there was a trace of excitement in his voice. 'There seems to've been a murder . . . '

'Murder?' ejaculated Hawkins incredulously.

'Yes, sir,' said the sergeant. 'A man named Brinn was found stabbed to death in the garden.'

Hawkins stared at him.

'You're quite sure of this?' he demanded. 'It's not somebody playing a joke?'

'No, sir,' answered the sergeant, shaking his head, 'the young lady was very upset . . . '

'Young lady?' broke in Hawkins.

'Miss Hatton, sir,' explained the man.

'It was she who rang, sir.'

'I'll go along at once,' said Hawkins. 'Is Archer in?'

The sergeant nodded.

'I'll take him with me,' said the superintendent. 'You'd better get on to Doctor Swinley. Ask him to meet me at the house. Get Archer to fetch the car round here.'

'I've got mine outside,' put in Mr. Budd. 'I'll run you to this place.'

'That's fine,' agreed Hawkins with alacrity. 'Never mind about the car, then, sergeant. Funny this should have happened,' he went on, when the sergeant had gone, 'just when I was saying how quiet everything was . . . '

'Who's this man Criller?' asked Mr. Budd.

'Rather an unpleasant chap,' said Hawkins. 'Rich as the devil and as mean as blazes. His niece is a nice girl, very pretty, but he treats her like dirt. Most people hate him in the village.'

'Has he lived here long?'

'About ten years. It might be a bit more or a bit less but it's round about that time.'

'What about this man, what was his name?' began Mr. Budd.

'Brinn,' interpolated Hawkins.

'What about him?' went on Mr. Budd. 'Is he a member of Criller's household?'

The local man shook his head.

'No, I don't know who he is,' he answered. 'Probably a friend of the old man's — if he's got any friends, which seems impossible to me.'

He pulled on his overcoat and they went out to Mr. Budd's ancient car. Hawkins eyed it dubiously.

'Maybe it'ud be better if we got the police car after all,' he began, but Mr. Budd cut him short.

'There's nothin' wrong with my car,' he said firmly. 'It may not look like one o' these new models, but it goes.'

Hawkins pursed his lips.

'All right. Get in,' he said to the constable who was waiting. 'I'll risk it.'

He squeezed himself in beside Mr. Budd and they started. The car certainly went, as the stout superintendent had said, but it was by no means a smooth journey. Hawkins had never heard so many rattles and squeaks from a car before.

The fact that it ever got them as far as their destination without blowing up was a source of wonder to Hawkins for many weeks afterwards. But it did. Following the local superintendent's directions, Mr. Budd brought them to the end of the lane that led to the white gate of Mr. Criller's house.

'You'll have to stop here and walk the rest of the way,' said Hawkins. 'The lane's too narrow for a car.'

Mr. Budd pulled up with a protesting squeal from the brake drums, and got heavily out. He followed Hawkins and the constable along the narrow path, through the gate, and up to the front door.

A neatly dressed maid opened it in answer to the local superintendent's ring. He introduced himself and asked for Mr. Criller.

'Will you wait here, please,' said the girl in a scared voice, ushering them into the hall. She closed the front door and left them standing while she went to the end of the lobby and disappeared through a door on the right. After a few minutes she came back.

'Will you come into the study, please,' she said. 'Miss Hatton will see you in a moment.'

Grace only kept them waiting a few seconds. She came in looking completely self-possessed and greeted them coolly. Only the slight trembling of her hands showed the strain under which she was labouring.

'My uncle has gone to his room,' she said. 'The shock rather upset him, but when you wish to see him he'll come down.'

'Thank you, miss,' said Hawkins. 'Perhaps you could tell us briefly what has happened?'

She complied at once. Her voice was quite steady as she recapitulated her grim discovery earlier, but none of them guessed what an effort it cost her.

'It seems an extraordinary business,' commented Hawkins when she had finished. 'I suppose you've no idea who could have killed this man?'

She shook her head.

'Not the slightest,' she replied truthfully.

'Does Mr. Criller suspect anyone?'

Again she shook her head.

'I don't think so,' she said.

Hawkins pursed his lips.

'It's a very queer business,' he muttered. 'It isn't as if the dead man was a resident. He was only on a visit. Who could have known that he was going to the summerhouse?'

Nobody answered him.

The point had struck Mr. Budd, too. So far as he could see the only people who could have known were the members of Mr. Criller's household. Officially, however, he had nothing to do with the case so he kept this suggestion to himself.

'Well,' remarked Hawkins, 'I'd like to see the body now. Will you show us the way, miss?'

She went over to the French windows and opened them.

'This is the quickest way,' she said, and they followed her out across the lawn.

'There's no need for you to come, if it

will upset you, miss,' said Hawkins kindly. 'Just show us which way from here.'

'Thank you,' she said gratefully. They had reached the beginning of the twisting path, and she pointed. 'If you follow that along you'll come to the summer-house . . .'

She was turning to go back when Mr. Budd caught sight of something white that was partially hidden by an over-growing laurel. It lay at the side of the path, and stooping with difficulty, he picked it up.

It was a handkerchief and, judging from the size, a man's handkerchief. The linen was of good quality and in one corner was a monogram.

'Know anybody with the initials J. L.?' he asked.

Grace stared at him dumbly. The only person she knew whom those initials fitted was Jim Longdon!

She felt the blood draining away from her cheeks. By an effort she regained control of her emotions, and her hesitation was barely perceptible before she replied:

'No, I don't know anyone with those initials.'

The instant she had spoken she regretted her denial. Superintendent Hawkins knew Jim. He would guess to whom that handkerchief belonged. She felt herself go hot and cold and hastily tried to rectify her error.

'At least,' she went on quickly, 'I don't think I do. May I see it, please?'

She held out her hand and Mr. Budd gave her the handkerchief. There was no doubt that it was one of Jim's. She recognised the monogram at once.

'I think,' she said slowly, 'that this must belong to Mr. Longdon.'

'I was just going to suggest that, miss,' said Hawkins. 'As soon as I heard the initials I thought of Mr. Longdon. I didn't know anyone else in this neighbourhood they'd fit.'

Mr. Budd saw her agitation and was curious. For the moment, however, he refrained from any comment.

'Longdon?' he repeated sleepily, turning his head towards Hawkins. 'Isn't that the name of the people whose house

Whipper burgled?'

Hawkins nodded.

'That's right,' he answered. 'I didn't know that he was a friend of Mr. Criller's . . . '

'He isn't,' put in Grace quickly. 'He's a friend of mine.'

Her face had gone very red, and the local superintendent noticing it, put her embarrassment down to a different cause.

'In that case,' he said cheerfully, 'the handkerchief's not going to prove much value to us.'

He continued on his way along the path, and Grace was hoping that the incident was over when Mr. Budd held out a podgy hand.

'I think I'd better keep that, miss, if you don't mind,' he said, and rather reluctantly she gave him the crumpled square of linen. Carefully he put it away in his inside pocket.

'When was Mr. Longdon here last?' he asked gently.

She hesitated.

'I — saw him last night,' she replied.

'Last night, eh?' Mr. Budd thoughtfully

massaged the lowest of his many chins. 'What time last night?'

'A little after half past nine,' she answered.

'I s'pose he came to the house?' murmured the stout man, and she shook her head.

'No,' she replied in a low voice. 'Mr. Criller doesn't like him very much. I met him out.'

'An' he came back with you, eh?' said Mr. Budd, nodding slowly. 'I see. You stood talking or walked somewhere near the end of this little path?'

She saw the trap he was leading her into and her mind worked quickly. Unless Jim had been somewhere near the path that led to the little summerhouse on the previous night he could not have dropped his handkerchief there. That was what this stout, sleepy-eyed man was trying to get out of her.

'Yes,' she lied. 'We stood talking here for quite a while.'

His sleepy eyes surveyed her but his face was inscrutable. She had no means of telling what he was thinking.

'I hope you don't mind me askin' these questions, miss,' he remarked almost apologetically. 'It's just as well to make sure how that handkerchief came to be there, isn't it?' He gave her a pleasant smile and turned away. She watched him as he vanished from sight round a turn in the path.

Mr. Budd walked on ponderously towards the summerhouse, and the expression on his face was puzzled. The girl was hiding something, there was no doubt in his mind about that. The finding of the handkerchief had been a shock to her. Although she had suggested a reason for its presence there, he was not at all convinced. If she were speaking the truth, why was she so obviously embarrassed? By the time he reached the summerhouse and joined Hawkins and the constable, Mr. Budd had decided that, if he were investigating the case, he would have the movements of Jim Longdon very carefully checked.

He found Hawkins staring at the huddled figure in the chair, and the superintendent looked round as Mr.

Budd paused at the foot of the steps.

'He's quite dead,' he announced.

The stout man nodded, entered the tiny rustic hut, and came over to his friend's side.

'Not any doubt that it was murder, eh?' he remarked. 'Look at his face.'

The dead man's face was distorted into an expression of terror such as he had seldom seen before.

'He saw death coming an' he was afraid,' he said. 'So afraid that he could neither cry out nor move.' He stretched out his arm and prodded gently with a fat forefinger at one of the dead man's arms. 'Stiff as a board,' he murmured. 'An' look at his hands — gripped tightly on the arms of the chair.'

'You think he knew the person who killed him?' asked Hawkins.

Mr. Budd nodded.

'I'm pretty sure he did,' he replied. 'He may not have known him when he first saw him, but he knew him before he died. It was what put that look on his face.'

He stared down at the table.

'What do you make of that?' he asked,

pointing to the rough 'S' that had been scrawled in the dead man's blood.

'What do *you* make of it?' said Hawkins.

'I don't make anythin' of it,' said Mr. Budd, rubbing the side of his nose. 'It was made by somebody's finger dipped in the dead man's blood. It could be somebody's initial.'

'Perhaps Criller will be able to explain it,' grunted the local superintendent. 'This man was a friend of his.'

He made a careful search of the little summerhouse, while the constable and Mr. Budd watched him, but he found nothing helpful. Just as he finished Doctor Swinley arrived. He was a small man, almost as fat as Mr. Budd but lacking his size. His face was round and red and jovial, and he had a ready smile which even the presence of violent death failed to suppress.

He greeted Hawkins cheerily.

'Got your message,' he said, clearing his throat, and dropping his bag on the floor. 'Came along as quickly as I could. This the corpse, eh? H'm, nasty — very nasty.' He stared down at the body and cleared his throat again. 'If it wasn't for the knife you'd think he died of sheer fright, eh?' He bent down and made a quick examination, muttering to himself all the while. 'H'm, well,' he said at length, 'I can't tell you very much. There will have to be an autopsy, of course. All I can tell you at the moment is that the knife went straight through the heart and death must have been instantaneous. Will that do?'

'How long would you say he'd been dead, doctor?' asked Hawkins.

'Difficult to say with any accuracy,' answered Swinley 'Might be an hour, might be two, certainly not more.'

He pulled his nose between a forefinger and thumb.

'Get the body to the mortuary as soon as you can,' he continued. 'I'll get busy on it and let you have the result, eh? Must be off now.' He grinned broadly, nodded, and, almost before they realised he had gone, was bustling away down the path.

'We'll go up and have a word with the household,' said Hawkins. 'You stop here,

Archer, and wait for the ambulance.'

The constable saluted, and, leaving him on guard, they walked up towards the house.

Grace was waiting for them in the study. There was no sign of her former agitation, and when the local superintendent informed her that he would like to see Mr. Criller she nodded quietly and went over to the door.

'I'll tell him,' she said.

'Look here, Budd,' said Hawkins, when she had gone, 'I'm going to get on to the Chief Constable and report this murder. Now, I know him well enough to be pretty certain that he'll want to call in the Yard. As you're on the spot you'll probably get the job. I'd rather work with you than a stranger.'

'Interestin' an' peculiar,' murmured Mr. Budd. 'There is somethin' very queer about this business.'

'That's what I think,' agreed Hawkins. He pulled the telephone towards him and gave a number. In a few seconds he was connected and speaking rapidly with the man at the other end of the wire.

41

'That's that,' he remarked presently, hanging up the receiver. 'I've explained to the Chief Constable that you're here, and he's getting straight on to the Yard.'

Mr. Budd sighed.

'Well, if you insist on draggin' me into this, you will,' he said dolefully, but Hawkins knew that he was pleased. 'How long is this feller, Criller, goin' to be?'

Mr. Criller came in almost as he finished speaking, a trembling, decrepit figure. Mr. Budd, surveying sleepily the yellowish-grey tinge of the thin face, and the drawn look of the deep-set eyes, came to the conclusion that the shock of Brinn's sudden death had been a very severe one.

'Very sorry to trouble you, sir,' said Hawkins, as the old man walked unsteadily across to his desk and sat down, 'but I'm afraid we shall have to ask you one or two questions . . .'

He was interrupted by a tap on the door and the maid entered with a letter on a small salver. She handed this to Mr. Criller.

'I just found this in the box, sir,' she said.

The old man snatched it off the tray and glowered at it.

'I don't know the writing,' he muttered. 'Who can it be from? It's been delivered by hand . . . '

He turned it this way and that in his bony fingers, and then, with a grunt, tore it open. Withdrawing the single sheet of paper it contained, he unfolded it . . .

One glance at it he gave and then with a strangled cry he fell forward across the desk, his hands clawing at the mass of papers that covered the broad top.

3

Mr. Budd thought at first that the old man had had a stroke when he helped him up and saw his congested face and bloodshot eyes. But it proved to be nothing as serious as that, for, after sitting up for a moment and breathing heavily, Mr. Criller turned to Hawkins.

'Brandy!' he croaked hoarsely. 'Get me some brandy! In the dining room . . . ' His voice cracked and he swallowed with difficulty.

The local superintendent hurried away, and the old man passed a shaking hand across his forehead.

'I'll be all right . . . in a minute,' he mumbled. 'My heart . . . not so strong . . . It gave me a shock . . . '

'The letter?' murmured Mr. Budd softly.

The old man nodded, opened his mouth as though he were going to speak, but said nothing.

'May I see it?' asked Mr. Budd.

Again the old man nodded.

'Yes, yes,' he said. 'Read it. It's probably a lot of tomfoolery, but it gave me a shock . . . At my age . . . ' His voice trailed away incoherently and he muttered something below his breath.

Mr. Budd stretched out a plump hand and picked up the single sheet of paper from the blotting-pad where it had fallen from Mr. Criller's nervous fingers. There was neither address nor date and the message had been written in capitals with a very black lead pencil. It ran:

'Brinn has gone. You will be the next. I put the warning on your gate last night.'

That was all. Where the usual signature should have been there was a roughly scrawled 'S' in red ink.

'Who sent you this?' asked the stout superintendent when he had read it twice.

'How should I know?' snarled Mr. Criller irritably. He was rapidly recovering. His voice was almost back to its normal strength.

Mr. Budd guessed that he was lying. That brief message held a very real significance for the old man, and, if he did not actually know the identity of the sender, he was in possession of information that would go a long way towards clearing up the mystery surrounding the murder of Franklin Brinn.

'What's all this about a warning on your gate?' he asked.

'Some fool scrawled an 'S' in red chalk on my gate last night,' grunted Mr. Criller.

'Why? What does this 'S' stand for?' inquired the big man, gently massaging his fleshy chin.

'I don't know. I know nothing about it at all,' snapped the other impatiently.

'You can say that,' thought Mr. Budd, 'but it isn't true.'

Hawkins came back at that moment with a glass partly filled with brandy. The old man seized it eagerly and gulped it down.

'That's better,' he growled, setting down the glass and wiping his lips with his handkerchief. 'But I still feel a bit shaky. I'm afraid you'll have to excuse me. I'm not in a fit state to answer any questions at the moment.' Gripping the edge of the desk he pulled himself to his feet and walked unsteadily to the door. 'I'm going to lie down for an hour,' he announced with his hand on the knob. 'After that I shall be at your disposal.'

He went out, closing the door after him, and Hawkins looked at the big man inquiringly.

'What's the matter with him?' he asked. 'What was in that letter?'

Mr. Budd handed him the message. Hawkins glanced at it and pursed his lips in a silent whistle.

'This looks as if the person who killed Brinn is after Criller, too,' he said.

'And he knows it,' said Mr. Budd softly. 'That's why he was so scared.'

'Did you ask him about it?'

'I asked him, but I couldn't get any sense out of him. He pretends that he doesn't know anythin'. That's a lot o' bunk, of course. He knows, all right. That's why he's pretendin' he's too ill to answer any questions. He wants time to think up a plausible story.'

Hawkins frowned.

'Meanwhile,' he said, 'the murderer's gaining time, too, to make a getaway . . . '

'I don't think it'll make much difference to that,' remarked the stout man, and Hawkins looked at him sharply.

'What do you mean by that?' he demanded.

'I mean, he hasn't finished his work yet,' answered Mr. Budd. 'It's my opinion that the warnin' in that note is genuine.'

'You mean he's after Criller?' said Hawkins.

Mr. Budd nodded slowly.

'Yes,' he said. 'And Criller knows it. If ever there was a man in fear for his life, that man's Criller.'

'Then why, in the name of sanity, doesn't he tell us all he knows?' exclaimed the local superintendent. 'If he's frightened of someone he must know who that someone is. Why not tell us, so that we can take steps to protect him?'

'Maybe, he's got a good reason,' said Mr. Budd.

Hawkins grunted something that was entirely uncomplimentary to Mr. Criller.

'Perhaps he isn't quite right in the

head,' he said aloud. 'Well, we'd better get on. We'll see if there's anything to be learned from the servants and Miss Hatton.'

He sent for Grace and questioned her thoroughly, but she could tell him very little. Franklin Brinn had been in the habit of paying more or less regular visits to the house each year. He had been connected with the various companies in which Mr. Criller was interested. His visits had been purely business ones. She remembered the incident of the chalked 'S' on the gate on the previous night, but could offer no explanation for it. Mr. Criller hadn't appeared to be very upset when he had seen it. She couldn't recollect anybody among his acquaintances with that initial.

They let her go at length and interviewed the servants. There were four of them. The housemaid, the kitchenmaid, the housekeeper, and the cook. From none of these did they learn anything of value.

They all knew Franklin Brinn and none of them liked him. The kitchenmaid had seen him cross the lawn and turn into the path to the summerhouse. She was able to state the time. It had been two minutes to one. She knew this because she had looked at the clock on the kitchen wall.

Nobody remembered seeing any stranger about the place that morning, because they had all been busy in the kitchen.

When they had all been dismissed, Hawkins looked at Mr. Budd and shrugged his shoulders dubiously.

'Not much there,' he remarked ruefully.

'No,' answered the big man. He yawned. 'Criller's the only person who can really tell us anythin' . . . '

'Let's see if he's better now,' said Hawkins, and rang the bell.

The housemaid answered it and was dispatched, reluctantly, to find her master. She came back in a few minutes to say that he was not in his room.

'He must be somewhere in the house,' said Hawkins. 'See if you can find him, miss.'

But he was not in the house.

While they had been interviewing the

servants, Mr. Criller had slipped quietly away, and where he had gone none knew.

★　★　★

Sir Benjamin Gottleib first saw the light of day — or as much of it as was left after it had filtered through the grime of the windows — in a dingy room over his father's pawnshop off the Whitechapel Road.

He was an ugly baby. His mother, after one glance at him, suffered a relapse, and his father declared that he was no son of his, and stoutly maintained this to the day of his death.

When he was twenty-five his father died, leaving his son the small pawnbroking business and the care of his mother. For two years young Gottleib devoted himself heart and soul to the business and made it a more profitable concern than his father had ever done. At the expiration of that time, his mother died, and the young man, who was tired of the pawnshop and wished to launch out into bigger things, sold the whole thing, lock, stock, and barrel, for five thousand pounds.

With this capital he opened a 'bucket' shop, and his shrewdness doubled his capital in eighteen months. From that moment he never looked back. People said of him that he could not make a mistake; that he never touched anything that wasn't successful. There were others who said unkinder things, but they were the people from whom he made his living and were naturally prejudiced.

It was a maxim of his that anything in the world could be bought if you paid enough for it. He had acquired all he had in this way. His association with Mr. Criller had added nearly a quarter of a million to his already swollen coffers, and with part of this he purchased a title and settled down in the country.

At the age of sixty-three he was a fat, heavy-jowled man, with an unpleasant face and a perpetual scowl, not unlike a bald, clean-shaven, gorilla.

Ten years before, he had married an anaemic member of the aristocracy whose father had willingly handed over his daughter instead of repaying the loan which he had owed to Mr. Gottleib for the greater part of five years.

The lady was thin and acid-faced, and frankly loathed her plebeian husband. The small amount of blue blood which she possessed in her veins dried up after three years of married life, and she died one night, peacefully in her sleep.

The marriage had been childless, much to the annoyance of Mr. Gottleib, who wanted a son. In order to repair the inadequacies of nature, he adopted one of his clerks who was an orphan, and the small amount of affection that he had in his ugly and unprepossessing body he lavished on this young man.

Percy Gottleib — he took his benefactor's name at the time of his adoption — was a thin, weedy youth of twenty, with light-coloured hair and a supercilious expression that people who knew him found very irritating. No work, and more money than was good for him, were having their effect on a character already weak, and if Percy Gottleib was not quite a degenerate, he had not very far to go.

He was standing in the ornate library at Dene Close, arguing with his foster-father, when a servant announced Mr. Criller.

'What's 'e want?' said Gottleib irritably. In spite of his money he had always found his 'H's' difficult to manage.

'He wants to see you, sir,' answered the manservant. 'He said it was urgent.'

'I suppose I'd better see 'im,' grunted Gottleib. 'Show 'im in 'ere.'

The servant withdrew, and Gottleib turned to the pasty-faced youth who stood by his desk.

'You clear out, Percy,' he ordered. 'I'll talk to yer later.'

The young man obeyed sullenly, and he had barely left the room before Mr. Criller was ushered in through the other door. The old man's sallow face was faintly flushed and he was breathing heavily. He had walked the distance that separated his own house from Dene Close, and it was a considerable distance for a man of his age.

'Well, Criller,' greeted Gottleib a little ungraciously when they were alone. 'What the devil do you want, eh?'

The old man sank into a huge easy chair and wiped his damp face.

'I want your advice,' he said unsteadily. 'Brinn came to see me this morning. He's dead.'

Sir Benjamin Gottleib shrugged his shoulders.

'What's that got ter do with me?' he demanded. 'I always thought 'e'd pop off sudden. 'E ate too much an' drank too much . . . '

'He didn't die naturally,' broke in Mr. Criller. 'He was murdered . . . '

The long cigar fell from Gottleib's fingers and hit the desk with a little shower of sparks.

'Murdered?' he repeated sharply. 'How? When?'

'He was stabbed — this morning,' answered Mr. Criller. 'In the summer-house in my garden.'

The other eyed him suspiciously.

'Is this a joke you're tryin' ter pull on me?' he demanded.

'Am I laughing?' snarled the old man. 'D'you think I'd've come all this way to amuse you? It's the truth . . . '

The big, ugly face of Gottleib was grey.

'Brinn must've made a lot of enemies,' he muttered.

''E was mixed up in all sorts o' shady things . . .'

'I haven't told you all yet,' interrupted Mr. Criller. 'On the table in front of him someone had scrawled a capital 'S' in his blood . . .'

With a startled oath, Gottleib sprang to his feet.

'What's that?' he cried huskily. 'You're lyin', Criller. You're tryin' to frighten me . . .'

'Don't be a fool!' snapped the old man angrily. 'Why should I try an' frighten you? I'm not in my second childhood. I'm telling you the truth . . .'

'It ain't possible,' muttered Gottleib, pacing up and down the big room with short, jerky steps. 'After all these years . . .'

The old man's lips curled into a sneering smile. For a moment he had forgotten his own fear in his enjoyment of his friend's agitation.

'That's what I thought,' he grunted, 'but I've had confirmation since that I was wrong.'

Rapidly he told the other about the mark on the gate and the message he had received a short while ago. Gottleib listened with increasing alarm.

'There's no doubt,' he said. 'There can't be any doubt. An' I thought that was all over an' done with . . . '

'So did I?' agreed Mr. Criller. 'What are we going to do, eh? We're both in danger. They've got Brinn, and they mean to get me. After that it'll be your turn. What are we going to do?'

Gottleib stopped beside his desk. For a moment he stared down at the blotting-pad with knitted brows. Then he looked round.

'I'm surprised you didn't realise the meaning of that mark on the gate,' he said slowly, drumming with his stubby fingers on the back of the writing chair.

'Well, I didn't, and that's that,' snarled the old man. 'I'd forgotten . . . I thought it had been done by some of the village boys. They'd do anything to annoy me. They all hate me round here . . . '

'Who d'you think's at the bottom of this?' asked Gottleib suddenly. Criller shrugged his shoulders.

'Do you think I'd be wasting my time here, if I did?' he said. 'Of course, I don't. It can't be Singleton, he's dead. We know that.' The glance he gave the other was significant. 'But it must be someone who knows all about that business.'

'Singleton had friends an' relations,' said Gottleib, licking his lips. 'What 'appened to 'em?'

'I don't know,' answered the old man. 'He had a wife and son, didn't he?'

The other nodded.

'Yes,' he replied thoughtfully. 'The son was eighteen.' He made a rapid mental calculation. 'He'd be thirty-eight now. P'raps he's behind this?'

'Anyone who was connected with Singleton may be behind it,' snarled the old man irritably. 'What's the good of conjecturing? What we've got to do is to take steps to protect ourselves . . . '

'We can go to the police,' began Gottleib, but the other stopped him with an oath.

'Are you crazy?' he demanded. 'We can't go to the police without telling them the truth, and if we do that we'll find ourselves on trial for murder . . . '

'I wasn't suggestin' that we should tell 'em the truth,' broke in Gottleib. 'I've got a bit o' sense, ain't I? Between us we ought ter be able to hatch up a story that'd look good.'

Mr. Criller's eyes narrowed.

'There's something in that,' he admitted grudgingly. 'What could we tell 'em that 'ud sound plausible?'

Gottleib helped himself to another cigar, lit it, and began to walk up and down the room again.

'How about somethin' like this,' he said, after a moment or two. 'It ought ter do the trick . . . '

For the next half an hour he talked rapidly while Mr. Criller listened, interpolating a suggestion every now and again.

'Yes,' he agreed at last. 'I think that might do. Yes, we might get away with it . . . '

When he left his step was more certain and his bearing more assured than when he had arrived.

As he left the library by one door, the

weedy form of Percy Gottleib straightened itself from outside the other. There was a peculiar expression on his unpleasant face as he moved softly away. He had heard all that had passed between the two men, and it had given him cause for much intensive thought.

4

The woman who stood at the big window, staring out across the lawn, had once been beautiful. Even now, in spite of the iron-grey hair and lined face, traces of that beauty still remained in the dark eyes, the wellshaped nose, and the small mouth.

The view that stretched before her was a pleasant one. Beyond the trim lawn was a thick belt of shrubbery, backed by stately trees, their branches now gaunt and leafless. The well-kept flower beds that flanked the lawn were ablaze with massed chrysanthemums — great golden, white, and rust-red blooms that flamed in the pale sun.

But Helen Longdon saw little of the beauty that lay before her. Her mind had gone back into the distant past and her thoughts were unhappy ones.

The sound of the door opening roused her from her reverie, and she looked round as her son entered.

'Hello, Jim,' she said, and her face broke into one of its rare and lovely smiles. 'Just got back?'

He nodded, crossed over to an easy chair, and dropped into it. She came and sat down opposite him.

'A terrible thing happened this morning,' he said. 'There's been a murder at Criller's . . . '

'I know,' she broke in quietly.

'You know?' He stared at her in astonishment. 'How do you know?'

'Somebody told me,' she answered. She took a cigarette from a box on the table beside her chair, and twisted it about in her white fingers. 'It was one of the servants, I think. It was Franklin Brinn, wasn't it?'

Jim nodded. He took out a lighter, flicked it into flame, and lit his mother's cigarette.

'He was stabbed in the little summer-house in Criller's garden,' he said.

Helen Longdon smiled, but it was a different smile to the one with which she had greeted his entrance. There was no loveliness in it — only a cold and sardonic satisfaction.

'He, at least, has got his deserts,' she said. 'I wonder when Criller and Gottleib will get theirs?'

'It's a pretty terrible way to die,' said Jim.

She blew out a thin stream of smoke and looked at him steadily.

''An eye for an eye, a tooth for a tooth, a life for a life,'' she said, speaking almost to herself. 'That's what we were taught when we were young. It applies as much today as it ever did.'

'Nothing can justify murder,' he protested.

'Was it murder to kill Franklin Brinn?' she demanded harshly. 'Would it be murder to take the lives of Criller and Gottleib? I wonder?'

'It's murder to kill any human being . . .' he began, but she stopped him with a gesture.

'They are not human,' she said. 'Parasites, preying on their fellow creatures, whose one object is the amassing of wealth — not because of the pleasure it can bring to themselves or others, but just because it is wealth. To rid the world of such people might, in the eyes of the law, be murder, but to me it would be merely an act of justice.'

Her son moved uneasily in his chair. His mother was in one of the moods he hated.

'I know we have good cause to hate all three of them,' he said. 'But it's still a terrible thing for a man to be killed suddenly, like Brinn was, without a chance . . .'

'Did he ever give anyone a chance?' asked his mother. 'Did he give your father a chance? No! He, and the others with him, gave your father no more chance than the person who struck him down gave Brinn.'

The entrance of the maid with tea prevented the reply that hovered on Jim's lips. There was a silence while the girl set down the tray and withdrew.

'You must be ready for some tea,' said Mrs. Longdon, and her voice was even once more. No trace of the emotion that had shaken it a few moments before remained.

'I am,' he answered. He watched his mother's slender hands moving among the tea things with relief. He was grateful for the interruption, for he had no wish to listen to a subject which had been discussed countless times before; no wish to receive confirmation of the fear which gnawed at his mind.

'Have you seen Grace today?' asked Mrs. Longdon as she handed him a cup of tea.

He shook his head.

'Not today,' he answered. 'I saw her last night.'

'This will be rather unpleasant for her,' she said, stirring her tea. 'I don't suppose Criller will be in the best of tempers after what's happened.'

'Is he ever in the best of tempers?' asked Jim.

'No, but this will make him worse,' she replied. She picked up a silver knife and began to cut a cake into wedge-shaped portions. 'I wonder why that girl stays with him?'

Jim shrugged his shoulders.

'Not more than I do,' he said. 'I begged

her to leave him and marry me, you know that, but she won't hear of it.'

'She's a strange girl,' remarked Mrs. Longdon. 'I should have thought she would have welcomed the chance of getting away from him.'

'There's something queer, I think,' said her son. He reached forward and helped himself to a piece of cake. 'I believe that old devil's got some kind of hold on her. I'm sure she isn't happy.'

'You're most likely right,' agreed his mother. 'Nothing that Criller ever did would surprise me.'

She changed the subject abruptly and began to talk commonplaces. After a second cup of tea, Jim made an excuse and went up to his room. Shutting the door, he pulled a chair up to the electric fire, and gave himself up to his troubled thoughts.

Grace Hatton worried him a good deal, but at the moment she was not his greatest trouble. He had another and more pressing problem to deal with.

For a long time he sat motionless while the darkness of the November night gathered in the room. It was quite dark before he finally got up stiffly, stretched himself, and lighted a cigarette. His face looked pale and drawn when he switched on the light and drew the curtains over the windows. The dreadful possibility which had been with him ever since he had heard of the death of Franklin Brinn had not yielded to reason.

If anything, it had assumed larger proportions — a fearful shadow that hung like a cloud over the house which would allow him no peace of mind until it had been dispelled . . .

★　★　★

Mr. Criller came back as suddenly as he had vanished. Mr. Budd and Superintendent Hawkins were discussing his disappearance when he walked in through the open French windows of the study. Without a word he went over to the writing table and sank down heavily in the chair.

'I felt in need of some air and exercise.'

He offered a brief and grudging explanation for his absence as he removed his hat and wiped his perspiring forehead.

'I wish you'd told us you were going out, sir,' said Superintendent Hawkins.

Mr. Criller looked at him coldly.

'Is it necessary that I should account for my actions to you?' he snapped.

Hawkins flushed and his mouth set.

'In the circumstances, yes, sir,' he answered stiffly, 'We're investigating a serious crime . . . '

The old man stopped him with an impatient gesture.

'I know — I know all that,' he retorted irritably. 'I fail to see how the fact that I left the house for a short period can interfere with your investigations. As a matter of fact, it was in connection with this dreadful business that I went out.'

Mr. Budd, who was lounging, apparently half asleep, in an easy chair, opened one eye.

'Now that's very interestin',' he murmured. 'How was it connected?'

Mr. Criller pulled at a loose piece of flesh under his chin.

'I think I may be able to throw some light on poor Brinn's death,' he said. 'There's something I haven't told you. I couldn't very well divulge it without first consulting my friend, Sir Benjamin Gottleib, since it concerned him as well as myself . . . ' He paused and cleared his throat.

The stout superintendent watched him expectantly.

What was it this unpleasant old man was going to reveal? He had thought all along that Mr. Criller knew more about the crime than he had seen fit to tell them.

'Mind you,' continued Mr. Criller, rolling a pencil up and down his blotting pad, 'what I'm going to tell you happened a long time ago. It may not have any bearing on this matter at all. Brinn's death and the mark on the table may be just a coincidence. That is for you to judge.'

He paused and seemed to be searching his mind for the best way to begin.

'This episode which I'm going to relate,' he went on presently, 'happened fifteen or sixteen years ago. Gottleib, poor Brinn, and myself were concerned with the flotation of a company concerned with a silver mine in Bolivia. One of the largest shareholders in this concern was a man named Charles Seton. He invested twenty thousand pounds in the company. Unfortunately it did not turn out as well as we had expected. The report on the mine was not justified and the company went into liquidation. Gottleib, Brinn, and myself, lost a considerable sum of money. I regret to say that Seton lost his twenty thousand pounds. Nobody was to blame. It was just one of those unfortunate things . . . '

He looked quickly from one to the other as though challenging them to refute this statement; but neither Mr. Budd nor Superintendent Hawkins said anything. They waited for him to continue.

'As I said,' went on the old man, 'nobody was to blame. But Seton seemed to imagine that he'd been tricked out of his money. There was no reason why he should think this, the reports and the books were all open for inspection, but he did, and he was very — well, unpleasant about the whole thing. First of all he threatened us with the law, but when it was pointed out to him that he had no grounds for taking the matter to court, he threatened other things. He was violently abusive and swore to get even with us. Although it happened so long ago, I remember his exact words; 'I'll get you first, Brinn,' he said, 'because it was you who persuaded me to invest in this swindle. After that I'll get Gottleib and Criller. I may have to wait a long time, but I'll get you all in the end,' he went raging out of the office and that was the last we ever saw of him.'

'And is it your belief,' remarked Mr. Budd slowly, 'that this man — Seton — is responsible for Brinn's death?'

'That's for you to decide,' said Mr. Criller shortly. 'I've told you what happened. That's all I can do.'

'I see,' murmured the big man. 'Now, supposin' that this incident with Seton is related to the murder, what d'you think is the meanin' of the 'S' scrawled on the table top? Seton's initial?'

'That seems obvious, doesn't it?' snarled the old man.

'So that Seton was advertisin' the fact that he'd killed this man?' said Mr. Budd. 'D'you think that's likely?'

'I don't think anything,' retorted Criller irritably. 'All I'm saying is that, so far as I know, Seton is the only person who had any motive for killing Brinn and writing me that letter.'

Mr. Budd settled himself more comfortably in his chair and gently rubbed the side of his nose.

'If you're right,' he said thoughtfully, 'it looks as though you an' this feller — what's-his-name? — Gottleib? are in danger too?'

'Has that only just occurred to you?' sneered Mr. Criller. 'Of course we are . . .'

Hawkins looked a little annoyed. This yellow-faced old man who sat glowering at them from behind his desk was very difficult to deal with. He controlled his temper, however, and when he spoke there was no trace of the anger he was feeling in his voice.

'Can you supply us with this man, Seton's, last known address and his description?' he inquired.

Mr. Criller hesitated.

'I can give you his description,' he said after a pause. 'As for his last address — well, I shall have to look that up. He was a man of medium height . . . '

'Just one moment, sir,' interrupted the local superintendent taking out a notebook and pencil. 'Now, sir . . . '

'He was a man of medium height,' repeated the old man. 'Rather on the stout side, and he wore glasses — spectacles . . . '

'Dark or fair?' asked Hawkins, jotting down the details.

'Dark,' answered the old man, 'very dark — and going a little bald . . . '

'Any peculiarities about him?' interpolated Mr. Budd.

Mr. Criller pursed his thin lips.

'I can't recollect any,' he said.

'What was his age?'

'It's difficult to say — between thirty-five and forty, perhaps. He may have been older . . . '

The description was vague. Mr. Budd looked at Hawkins. From the dubious expression on the superintendent's face he evidently thought so too.

'Can't you think of anything else that might help us trace this man, sir?' he asked.

'I'm afraid not,' answered the old man shaking his head. 'If anything occurs to me I'll . . . '

He was interrupted by the entrance of the housemaid.

'If you please, sir,' said the girl, 'Sir Benjamin Gottleib wants to see you at once.'

Mr. Criller frowned.

'What the devil does he want?' he growled. 'All right, show him in . . . '

But Benjamin Gottleib did not want showing in. He was already in. Shouldering his way past the girl, he strode up to the desk. His ape-like face was grey and moist, his ungainly body shaking as though with an ague.

'This is dreadful, Criller,' he cried huskily. 'Dreadful. Something must be done at once . . . '

'What's dreadful?' snarled the old man furiously. 'What's the matter with you?'

'This!' Gottleib fumbled in his pocket, produced an envelope, and with difficulty extracted a sheet of paper from it. 'Read that,' he cried excitedly. 'Read it! I found it in my letter box half an hour ago . . . '

He threw the sheet of paper in front of Mr. Criller. The old man stared down at it and his face puckered into a grimace of fear.

'God Almighty,' he whispered, in a voice that was only a croak. 'So you're going to be the next . . . '

'Let me see that,' broke in Mr. Budd curtly. With surprising swiftness he hoisted himself to his feet and came over to the desk. He picked up the sheet of paper and looked at it. A single line of writing had been roughly printed in pencil. It ran:

'*Brinn is dead. Tomorrow night at twelve you will die too.*'

Where the signature would normally have been was a scrawled 'S' in red ink.

Mr. Budd read the short message again. His face was completely devoid of any expression. There was no doubt that the note had been written by the same person who had sent the similar message to Mr. Criller. Both the paper and the pencil were similar.

Nodding his head slowly he passed the paper over to Hawkins.

'I've told them about Seton,' grunted Mr. Criller, and Mr. Budd, who missed nothing, thought there was something significant in the look he gave the other.

'Oh, yer 'ave, eh?' said Gottleib. 'Well, what d'you make of it?'

He looked at Hawkins and Mr. Budd and it was the latter who answered.

'Well,' he remarked ponderously, 'there may be somethin' in it, but there's very little for us to go on. You haven't seen this feller Seton for fifteen years or more, an' that's a long time. It seems funny to me that if he was goin' to get back on you for this business that happened so long ago, he didn't try it before.'

76

'There's nobody else it could be,' snapped the old man quickly. 'Seton is the only person who ever threatened us . . .'

'I don't care a damn who's responsible,' broke in Gottleib impatiently. 'The only thing that matters is we've been threatened. Something's got to be done about it . . .'

'Somethin' 'll be done about it all right,' said Mr. Budd soothingly. 'Don't you worry about that. Every precaution will be taken to see that this threat isn't carried out.'

The gorilla-like face was turned towards him, and Gottleib licked his lips.

'This note is more explicit than the other,' went on the stout man. 'It states a time — twelve o'clock tomorrow night.'

'That may be just to put us off,' suggested Hawkins. 'The danger may be any time . . .'

'Which means that we've got to start takin' steps to protect him from now on,' said Mr. Budd. 'We'll arrange for a special guard at once, an' take extra precautions at twelve o'clock tomorrow night. Can you arrange for that?'

Hawkins nodded.

'Yes,' he answered. 'If I can use your telephone, sir, I can arrange for a man to pick up Sir Benjamin when he leaves here and accompany him home. The man will remain on duty till nightfall when I'll send up another to relieve him.'

Mr. Budd nodded approvingly.

'That's fine,' he said.

'Can I use your phone, sir?' asked Hawkins again, glancing at Mr. Criller, and the old man gave a grudging consent.

The local superintendent gave a number, was connected, and after a few minutes' conversation hung up the receiver.

'That's fixed,' he announced. 'There'll be a constable here in a quarter of an hour, and he'll go back with you to your house.'

'What about me?' demanded Mr. Criller grumpily. 'It's all very well for Gottleib, but what about me? Am I to be left here alone at the mercy of this murderous scoundrel?'

'Constable Archer is already on guard

here, sir,' Hawkins pointed out. 'I'll see that another man takes his place when he goes off duty.'

'What we've got to do now,' remarked Mr. Budd, 'is to decide about tomorrow. If an attempt *is* made to get at Sir Benjamin at midnight, we ought to stand a very good chance of catchin' our man.'

He closed his eyes almost completely and there was a short silence.

'My suggestion is this,' he continued suddenly. 'We'll keep to the present arrangement until, say ten o'clock tomorrow night. At that time we'll go along to Sir Benjamin's house an' augment the original guard. How does that strike you?'

'It seems a good idea,' said Hawkins. 'I doubt very much if anything'll happen. This fellow, Seton, or who-ever-it-is, is sure to get wind of the guard, and unless he's a fool he'll keep away.'

'Why should he become aware that there's a special watch being kept?' demanded Mr. Budd. 'I don't see how he's to find out if we're careful. There's no reason why we shouldn't reach the house without anyone bein' the wiser. Sir

Benjamin will behave as usual . . . '

'May I make a suggestion,' put in Mr. Criller, raising his eyes from his blotting-pad.

'What is it?' grunted Gottleib.

'It's this,' said the old man. 'Instead of all this taking place at *your* house, it should take place here, at mine.'

Gottleib frowned.

'I don't see why,' he began.

'Don't you?' grunted Mr. Criller irritably. 'I'll explain more carefully. My suggestion is this: All of you come and dine with me here tomorrow night. You, Gottleib, arrange to stay the night. That'll have the effect of doing *two* things. First, if this man, Seton, has planned an attempt to take place at your house, it'll rather upset his plans if you aren't there, won't it? Secondly, it will supply *me* with some form of protection. This warning may have been sent as a blind so that you'll all concentrate on Gottleib and leave me unguarded and at the mercy of the killer.'

He looked from one to the other.

Mr. Budd smiled. There was no doubt

in his mind what the reason was which had prompted Mr. Criller's suggestion. It was an entirely selfish one. At the same time there was a modicum of sense in what he said. Hawkins was obviously in favour of it.

'It will have one great advantage,' he said. 'I shall be able to economise in men, and I've none too many. This is a small district and we're understaffed as it is.'

'I'm agreeable,' said Gottleib, and Mr. Budd thought, a little reluctantly. 'I must say I'd rather remain at me own 'ouse.'

'I didn't make the suggestion for the pleasure of your company,' snarled Mr. Criller, 'but because I'm rather concerned about my own safety. If you don't want to come, say so, but I shall insist on adequate protection . . . '

'I've said I'll come, ain't I?' snapped Gottleib angrily. 'I can see that it's safer for us to keep together. What a difficult feller you are, Criller.'

'Well, we'll fix it like that,' interposed Mr. Budd. 'Superintendent Hawkins an' me will come over in the mornin' an' arrange the final details.'

'All right,' said Gottleib. 'I must go now. See yer tomorrow.'

The constable Hawkins had sent for was waiting in the hall and Gottleib took his leave. Mr. Budd and Hawkins went with him. On the way down the path to his car, the local man gave the constable his instructions. Gottleib's chauffeur threw away the cigarette he had been smoking and opened the door for his master, and his eyes widened as the uniformed constable got in as well.

'By the way,' remarked Mr. Budd, as the car was on the point of moving away, 'about this feller, Seton. Can you give us a description of him?'

'But,' began Hawkins and stopped as the stout man nudged him.

'A description of Seton?' repeated Gottleib, and hesitated. 'I don't remember him very well. 'E was tall and a bit thinnish, fair hair with a reddish face. That's all I can remember.'

'Thank you,' said Mr. Budd, and chuckled as he saw the astonishment on Hawkins's face.

'Well, what d'you make of that?' gasped

the local superintendent as Gottleib's car drove away.

'Queer, isn't it?' remarked Mr. Budd. 'It rather confirms an idea I 'ad while Criller was tellin' his story.'

'What's that?' demanded Hawkins.

'That all this business about Seton is a fake,' answered Mr. Budd shaking his head sorrowfully. 'Just an invention on Criller's part an' Gottleib's too, of course, to throw dust in our eyes . . .'

'Do you mean the whole thing's a fake?' demanded his friend in astonishment. 'Those letters . . . ?'

'Oh, there's no fake about them,' interrupted the stout man. 'They're real enough. So is the fact that both these fellers, Criller an' Gottleib, are scared to death. But they're not scared of this chap, Seton. They're scared of someone else — the person who killed Brinn, an' signs 'is letters with a capital 'S' . . . ' He pursed his thick lips. 'They don't want us to know who that person is,' he went on. 'They want protection, but they don't want to tell us who from.'

'Why not?' demanded Hawkins.

Mr. Budd shook his head slowly.

'I can't tell yer that,' he replied. 'It's all very interestin' an' peculiar. But if I was one of them detectives what's always makin' guesses I'd say that there was somethin' behind all this business that might involve Criller an' Gottleib very seriously — with the law.'

5

It rained heavily during the night, and when Mr. Budd awoke on the following morning and looked out of the window of his bedroom, the sky was still grey and overcast, although it was no longer actually raining.

The inn where he had put up on Hawkins's recommendation was comfortable and he had slept soundly. This affair on which he was engaged looked likely to turn out one of the most difficult cases he had ever become associated with. A telephone message had come through from the Assistant Commissioner of the C.I.D. agreeing to the Chief Constable's suggestion that Mr. Budd should work with Superintendent Hawkins, and the morning's post brought his official authority.

After breakfast, when he had smoked one of his evil-smelling cigars, he made his way slowly down to the little police station and found Hawkins in his office.

'Hello,' greeted the local man. 'I hope you slept well?'

'I always sleep well,' answered Mr. Budd. 'The only trouble is that I never get enough sleep.'

His friend eyed him critically.

'I don't believe you're ever really awake,' he said. 'You're fat because you're lazy and you're lazy because you're fat. It's a vicious circle.'

'Don't let's drag personalities into the conversation,' said Mr. Budd wearily. 'Anythin' happened?'

Hawkins shook his head.

'Nothing special,' he answered. 'I've seen the coroner. The inquest on Brinn has been fixed for tomorrow at ten. Nothing happened at Gottleib's last night, I suppose?'

'Nothin' at all,' answered the big man. 'Let's fix up tonight. How many men are you bringin'?'

'Three,' said Hawkins. 'The man who's on guard at Gottleib's now, Archer and Bridges.'

'That makes five with you an' me,' murmured Mr. Budd. 'That should be enough.'

'I don't suppose anything'll happen,' said Hawkins. 'Unless the person who wrote that note is crazy, he'll guess that the police will've been notified.'

'Maybe,' said Mr. Budd, 'but we've got to take every precaution. I suggest that we go over an' pick up Gottleib about seven o'clock an' bring him to Criller's — or better still, you go an' fetch Gottleib an' I'll go to Criller's with Archer an' meet you there. How's that?'

'It's all right with me,' agreed Hawkins.

'We can make what other arrangements are necessary when the time comes,' said the stout superintendent. 'I think it'd be a good idea if two of the men were left to look after the outside of the house, while we, and the third, attend to the inside. The men outside can warn us if there's any sign of an unauthorised intruder.'

'That's quite a good idea,' said Hawkins.

'About this story of Seton,' Mr. Budd went on, 'I'll get on to the Yard and see if they can pick up any trace of him. I've no doubt they'll find that there is such a person, an' that he was associated with

87

one of Criller's enterprises. But I'm willin' to bet that he's not the person Criller an' Gottleib are afraid of.'

He put through his call, left the police station, and made his way up to Sir Benjamin Gottleib's house to keep his promised interview.

He found the unpleasant-looking Gottleib in his study talking to a weedy youth who looked equally unpleasant.

'This is my adopted son,' introduced Gottleib, and the weedy youth held out a limp and moist hand. 'I'm bringin' 'im with me tonight. I've told Criller and 'e don't mind.'

'Looks like being an exciting evening,' said Percy Gottleib languidly. 'I hope old Criller's dinner's good.'

Mr. Budd took an instant dislike to him. He hated his type and took very little pains to hide the fact. Rather pointedly ignoring the young man, he turned his attention to the elder Gottleib, and acquainted him with the arrangements he had discussed with Hawkins that morning.

Gottleib seemed satisfied. Although his

face was haggard and there were dark marks under his eyes, he appeared to be less fearful than he had been on the previous day. He was almost cheerful when he accompanied the stout man to the door and bade him good-bye.

Mr. Budd spent the rest of the day in getting acquainted with the district. After lunch, he got out his dilapidated car, and went for a long drive. It was late when he returned to the inn, had his tea, and went up to his room for a rest.

He reached the white gate leading to Mr. Criller's house, coincident with the arrival of Gottleib's big car containing its owner, the weedy youth, Superintendent Hawkins, and the two constables. They all walked up the path to the house together and were admitted by the housemaid.

Mr. Criller was standing in the hall, talking to Archer, when they arrived and he greeted them ungraciously as they shed their hats and coats.

'Come into the drawing room,' he grunted harshly. 'I suppose you'd like a drink?'

He opened a door across the hall and

ushered them into a big, shabbily furnished room that had the appearance of being seldom used.

Grace joined them just before eight, and Percy's small, red-rimmed eyes surveyed her appreciatively as she came in. The black dress she was wearing was a simple one — her allowance did not run to anything elaborate — but it served to set off the fairness of her skin, and accentuated, by contrast, the glory of her hair. She sat down quietly in a corner, and Percy edged his way unobtrusively round the room until he reached her side.

Mr. Criller, watching this manœuvre, gave a sardonic grin, and would probably have come out with a caustic comment but for the fact that dinner was announced at that moment.

They went into the dining room and sat down at the table, Percy Gottleib boldly seating himself next to the girl.

The meal which followed lingered long afterwards in Mr. Budd's memory. It was one of the most unpleasant he had ever attended. Their host was in his worst mood. He snapped and snarled at everybody, but in particular at Grace. Gottleib began to grow restless and uneasy, and started so violently, once, when the housemaid leaned over him to remove his plate, that he upset his glass, sending the wine streaming across the polished surface of the table.

He apologised gruffly, and the servant mopped it up. Grace was reminded vividly of the episode of the spilled port on the night before Franklin Brinn's death, and the old man's discomfort at the sight.

Only Superintendent Hawkins appeared to be free from the peculiar tenseness that everyone — including Mr. Budd — was feeling. He ate everything that was put before him, stolidly, saying little and seldom removing his eyes from his plate.

It seemed a very long time to Mr. Budd before the last course came to an end and Mr. Criller signified that coffee would be served in the study.

'You can go to bed,' he said to Grace as they rose. 'I shan't want you any more tonight. You'll only be in the way if you stay down here.'

She made no demur — Mr. Budd thought that she was rather relieved — but Percy uttered a protest.

'Oh, I say,' he exclaimed. 'I was hoping ... '

'You can mind your own business,' snarled Mr. Criller savagely. 'When I want you to run my house, I'll ask you!'

Percy's little eyes snapped dangerously. He opened his mouth to retort, but Gottleib nudged him and he remained silent, contenting himself with leering at the girl as she said good night and left them.

'Now,' said the old man, when they had congregated in the study, 'let's get to business. What are the arrangements for tonight?'

Mr. Budd told him what had been decided so far.

'The men outside the house have already taken up their positions,' he concluded. 'One is patrollin' the back an' the other the front. The third is in the hall. At the first sign of anythin' unusual they'll blow their whistles.'

'That seems all right,' grunted the old

man, nodding his bald head. 'But that's not all you're going to do, is it? You're not just going to sit round and wait, are you?'

'What else d'yer expect us to do?' demanded Gottleib irritably. 'Dance?'

'Don't be stupid,' snarled Mr. Criller. 'I think you ought to be isolated — for everybody's sake. I suggest that shortly before twelve we should all leave you in here, that the constable outside should be placed on guard at the window, that the door should be locked, and that Superintendent Budd and Superintendent Hawkins should take up their positions outside it . . . In these circumstances it will be impossible for anyone to get near you.'

He stopped and looked from one to the other to see how his suggestion had been received.

'Sounds all right,' said Gottleib. 'What do you say?'

He looked at Mr. Budd and Hawkins. They both nodded.

'I think it's a very sensible idea,' said the stout man, 'Provided the curtains at the window are drawn, just in case someone should try a shot from a distance. I don't see how anyone can get at you, sir, if this method is adopted. You agree, Hawkins?

'Yes, I agree,' said the local superintendent. 'It seems cast-iron.'

Mr. Criller's thin lips curled into a satisfied smile. Mr. Budd was under no illusions as to why he had made his suggestion. It was not because he was in the least interested in safeguarding his friend, but because, in the event of any trouble, it would give greater security to himself.

If any attempt should be made on Gottleib that night, the farther he was away from Criller the safer it would be for the old man. It had no doubt been this consideration that had inspired his plan.

★ ★ ★

At eleven o'clock Hawkins went out to give the two policemen their final instructions.

The rain, which had kept off during the day, had returned with the dropping of the wind, and a steady downpour was falling. The pattering of it on the leaves of the shrubbery was the only sound that disturbed the stillness of the night.

Neither Archer nor Bridges had anything to report. They had not heard or seen anything suspicious so far. The local superintendent marshalled them outside the study window and came back to the house.

During his absence, Mr. Criller and Percy had retired to the dining room, leaving Mr. Budd alone with Gottleib in the study. Now that the time mentioned in the warning was rapidly getting nearer, Gottleib began to show more and more signs of the strain under which he was labouring. His hand shook as he raised his cigar to his lips, and when he spoke his voice was husky and uncertain as though all the moisture in his throat had dried up.

The servants had already gone to bed. Mr. Budd, who was examining the fastening of the windows when Hawkins came in, suggested that he should make a tour of the lower part of the house in company with the inside constable to see that everything was securely locked up.

Hawkins agreed, and departed on this errand.

When he had gone, Mr. Budd pulled the heavy curtains over the windows, blotting out the sight of the two watchful policemen in their shining wet capes, and turned away.

'I don't see how it's possible for anythin' to happen to you,' he said to the shaking man in the desk-chair. 'The windows are securely fastened and bolted, an' when we leave you, an' you lock the door, it's impossible for any unauthorised person to get near you.'

'I 'ope yer right,' grunted Gottleib, and his face glistened in the light from the hanging pendant above the desk. 'I shall be damned glad when tonight's over, I can tell you.'

'I shan't be sorry myself,' said Mr. Budd. 'You've got nothin' to worry about. Sup'n'tendent Hawkins an' me an' the constable'll be in sight of the door all the time. An' those two p'licemen, outside, won't move from the window. To make

96

matters doubly sure you'd better call out 'all right' at intervals.'

'I'll call out all right,' said Gottleib fervently and mopped his face. It was obvious that with every passing second his fear was increasing, in spite of Mr. Budd's assurances and the precautions that had been taken. There was terror in his eyes, and his loose mouth twitched spasmodically.

The return of Superintendent Hawkins made him jump so violently that he dropped his half-smoked cigar, and had to grope under the desk to retrieve it. Hawkins reported that all the doors and windows were bolted and fastened. Mr. Budd looked at his watch.

It was half-past eleven.

In confirmation of this, the big clock in the hall chimed the half-hour.

'I think it's time we left you,' said Mr. Budd slowly. 'Don't forget, we shall listen for your call.'

Gottleib licked his lips and tried to answer, but his mouth and throat were dry, and he could only nod. They left him, and heard the key turn in the study door when they were outside. Leaving Hawkins to keep an eye on the closed door, Mr. Budd went across the hall and looked into the drawing room. Percy Gottleib was sprawled in an easy chair, fast asleep, while Mr. Criller glowered at him from the other side of the fireplace.

The old man looked up as Mr. Budd paused on the threshold.

'Hello,' he grated. 'What's happened? Gottleib died of fright?'

There was sneer in his voice and on his thin lips.

'No,' said the stout man. 'He's still alive and well. I came to see if you were all right.'

'I'm all right,' retorted the old man, 'except that I'm damned tired. D'you mind if I go to bed, if I want to?'

'You can please yourself about that,' answered Mr. Budd.

'Then I think I'll go now,' said Mr. Criller, struggling to his feet. 'I invariably go to bed at eleven-thirty — have done for years — and at my age it's difficult to break a habit.' He glanced at the sleeping Percy. 'Do him good if he did the same,' he added, and followed Mr. Budd out into the hall.

At the foot of the staircase, he left that portly man without a word of good night, climbed slowly up the stairs, and disappeared in the darkness of the upper landing.

Mr. Budd made a thorough inspection of the ground floor of the house, found everything as it should be, and joined Hawkins on the oak settle, from which they had a clear view of the study door. By the hall door the third constable was on guard.

The house was very silent. The gentle click-clack of the hall clock was the only sound that disturbed the stillness. Once only did they hear any other sound, when Gottleib called faintly from the study to inform them that he was all right.

Ten minutes more and it would be twelve o'clock — the hour at which the killer of Franklin Brinn had threatened to kill again.

Five minutes went slowly by, and then, intermingling with the steady ticking of the clock, came a sound that brought the sleepy-eyed Mr. Budd upright with a jerk. The next second he relaxed again and smiled. The sound he had heard developed into a long-drawn-out and unmusical snore that came from the direction of the drawing room. Percy Gottleib had apparently reached the noisy stage of his slumbers.

Slowly the minutes passed.

Mr. Budd found himself watching intently the long hand of the clock as it moved nearer and nearer to the perpendicular.

Two more minutes . . .

One . . .

There was a click and a faint whirring of wheels as the striking mechanism was released.

Dong!

The first stroke of twelve rang through the silence. In the midst of a particularly loud snore, Percy Gottlieb choked and gasped.

Dong!

The clock chimed twelve times and was silent.

Silent, too, was the man behind the

locked door of the study. No reassuring call came.

Mr. Budd waited for a full minute, and then he got heavily to his feet.

'He hasn't told us he's all right,' he muttered, staring anxiously at the closed door.

'Maybe, he's fallen asleep,' said Hawkins. 'I was nearly doing so myself when the clock struck.'

Mr. Budd lumbered over to the study door and hammered on it with his fist.

'Sir Benjamin,' he called. 'Sir Benjamin . . .'

But there was no reply.

He called again.

Still no answer.

Vainly, he tried the handle, but the door was still securely locked. He called the constable.

'Try your shoulder at it,' he ordered, and there was more than a touch of anxiety in his voice.

The constable lunged forward. His shoulder struck the panel and it cracked. But the door held firm.

'Again!' said Mr. Budd, and once more

the constable hurled his weight at the door. At the third attempt the lock gave. With a crash the door flew open, banging against the wall, as the screws of the lock tore out. Mr. Budd, Hawkins, and the panting constable, stared incredulously into the room.

Sir Benjamin Gottleib sat in the desk-chair, his wide-open eyes staring at the ceiling. Down his white face ran a trickle of blood that came from a small round hole in the centre of his forehead . . .

6

Mr. Budd was so staggered that, for a moment, he was unable to do anything except gape incredulously at what he saw.

He recovered almost at once, and leaving Hawkins still staring foolishly in the open doorway, went over to the motionless figure beneath the light and bent down.

Gottleib was dead!

He had been shot almost between the eyes that stared, sightlessly, at the ceiling. But they had heard no report — no sound at all . . .

Mr. Budd looked round.

'Phone for a doctor,' he ordered sharply. 'He's dead.'

Superintendent Hawkins found his voice and the use of his limbs.

'But it's impossible,' he muttered. 'Nobody could've got near him . . .'

'All the same, he's dead,' said Mr. Budd grimly. 'An' he couldn't've killed

103

himself or the weapon'd be here, an' there's no sign of it . . . '

He went over to the window. Pulling aside the heavy curtains, he looked out. It was still raining heavily and the wet capes of the two policemen outside gleamed blackly in the light.

They both looked round, startled at the sudden jerking back of the curtains. Mr. Budd, after making sure that the catch on the window had not been disturbed, opened it.

'You'd better come in,' he said curtly.

The two policemen entered wonderingly, and stood just inside the open window, little rivulets of water running from their capes and forming small pools on the carpet.

'Anythin' the matter, sir?' began Archer, and then, as he saw the dead man in the chair, stopped abruptly.

'There's quite a lot the matter,' said Mr. Budd. 'Sir Benjamin Gottleib has been killed.'

'Killed?' ejaculated the other constable. ''Ow was 'e . . . '

'He was shot,' answered Mr. Budd.

'How it was done, I don't know. Have you both been outside that window all the time?'

Archer nodded.

'We neither of us shifted at all, sir,' he replied.

'Did you hear any sound from inside here?'

'Not a thing, sir.'

Mr. Budd frowned.

The thing was impossible, and yet it had happened!

Apart from the two constables' testimony, he was prepared to swear that nobody had gained admittance by the window. The fastenings had not been tampered with and there were no marks on the floor which there must have been had anyone come in on such a wet night.

It was equally impossible that anyone could have entered by the study door. It had been securely locked, and both he and Hawkins had been watching it the whole time. Yet, in spite of the fact that the study had been practically hermetically sealed, Gottleib had been killed — shot.

It was unbelievable.

A sound from the doorway made the big man swing suddenly round. The weedy figure of Percy Gottleib appeared, yawning on the threshold.

'What's up?' he asked in a voice still husky with sleep. 'I woke up an' heard you all talking . . . '

'Don't come in,' broke in Mr. Budd. 'Go back to the drawing room . . . '

'Why? What's happened?' demanded Percy, and then his roving eyes saw the sprawling figure behind the desk.

They heard him catch his breath and saw the flush induced by sleep fade from his pasty face, leaving it a dirty grey.

'God Almighty!' The exclamation was an almost inaudible croak. 'How . . . has . . . ' The husky whisper trailed away to incoherence, and he stared with horrified eyes from one to the other of them, his loose lips moving soundlessly.

'Sir Benjamin is dead,' said Mr. Budd.

'How awful,' muttered Percy. 'What was it — heart attack?'

'He was shot,' answered the big man.

The small, red-rimmed eyes became

circles of astonishment.

'D'you mean — he was murdered?' he demanded shrilly. 'That the threat was carried out?'

'I'm afraid so,' said Mr. Budd.

'But how? Who did it?' asked the weedy youth, his eyes darting rapidly from one to the other.

'We don't know who did it — or even how it was done,' said Mr. Budd. 'I must ask you to go back to the drawin' room . . . '

Percy opened his mouth with the intention of saying something more, apparently thought better of it, and left them abruptly.

Hawkins roused himself from his condition of dazed wonder.

'I'll get the doctor,' he said and reached for the telephone.

He was a long time getting a reply to his call, but eventually he was successful.

'He's coming at once,' he announced, when he had finished his short conversation and replaced the receiver. He joined Mr. Budd who was examining the dead man in the chair.

The bullet had entered the head just between the eyes and there were no powder marks on the flesh. The shot, therefore, must have been fired from some distance away — at least six feet or more — and it had been fired in the room. Even now the hot-iron smell of burnt cordite lingered in the air.

But what had happened to the person who had fired the shot, and the weapon from which it had come, was a complete mystery.

Somebody had got into that room and killed Gottleib, but they had certainly not entered by the door or the window. Nor had they escaped by either of those means. That was an indisputable fact. There must, therefore, be some other means of entry.

The constables were dispatched to join the other one in the hall, and Mr. Budd and Superintendent Hawkins made a careful examination of the room. The walls, the floor, even the ceiling, were subjected to a close scrutiny, but without result.

There was no sign of any concealed

entrance, no hole that even a mouse could have got through, and at the end of their search they were faced with the incredible conclusion that unless the murderer had come by the door or the window, he could never have been in the room at all.

'Which,' declared Hawkins, shaking his head despairingly, 'is sheer nonsense. Unless Gottleib killed himself, somebody must have been in the room.'

'If he'd killed himself,' remarked Mr. Budd wearily, 'we'd've found the weapon.'

The arrival of Doctor Swinley prevented further conjecture and discussion for the time being.

'If this goes on,' remarked Swinley cheerfully, when he had heard what they had to say, 'we shall be getting notorious, eh? Two murders, one on top of the other, will make the news boys sit up.' He went over to the body. 'No doubt about his being dead,' he said, 'the bullet must've gone straight through the brain. I don't suppose he ever knew what killed him. H'm. Ha! There's no exit wound. The bullet's still in the head. Lodged in a bone, I expect . . . '

'That rather tends to show that the shot was fired from a distance, doesn't it?' asked Mr. Budd, and Swinley nodded.

'At least six feet, I should say,' he answered.

'We never heard the report,' said Hawkins.

'Silencer,' said Mr. Budd laconically. 'Must've been. We couldn't help hearing it otherwise.'

'It's a funny business altogether,' said Swinley. 'If you can make head or tail of it you're cleverer than I am, Gunga Din . . . '

There was a sudden altercation in the hall, and Mr. Budd went to the door to see what it was all about.

Mr. Criller, his thin body enveloped in a dressing gown over his pyjamas, was standing at the foot of the staircase arguing shrilly with Archer.

'How dare you order me about in my own house!' he cried angrily. 'If I wish to go into my study, I shall do so . . . '

'I'm sorry, sir,' said the constable

apologetically. 'I've got orders to see that . . . '

'The constable is only actin' on instructions,' interposed Mr. Budd gently.

'Whose instructions?' snarled the old man, glaring at him. 'I'm the only person who has the right to issue instructions in this house . . . '

'The instructions were mine,' retorted Mr. Budd. 'An' I've every right to issue 'em. A murder has been committed . . . '

'Murder?' squeaked Mr. Criller in alarm. 'Who's been murdered? Not Gottleib . . . ?'

Mr. Budd nodded gloomily.

'Who killed him?' demanded the old man. 'Have you got the person who killed him . . . ?'

He came over, clutching the dressing gown round his lean figure with a skinny hand.

'No, not yet,' said the stout superintendent. 'The whole thing's a bit difficult . . . '

'What were you all doing to let it happen?' snapped Mr. Criller accusingly. 'My God! You're a precious lot, aren't you? Five of you, and you go and let a man be killed under your noses . . . '

'Every precaution was taken,' said Mr. Budd. 'We could do no more than we did . . . '

'Precaution!' repeated the old man scathingly. 'Precaution? Bah! What good were your precautions when they had no effect, eh? Do you realise that I have been threatened too, and this murderous brute may turn his attentions to me?' His faded eyes blinked at them rapidly. 'How did it happen?' he went on. 'I demand to know how it happened?'

Mr. Budd told him. He listened, his hairless brows drawn together in a frown.

'Incredible,' he muttered. 'Ridiculous! There must have been some slackness somewhere.'

'There was no slackness,' said Mr. Budd. 'Every means of entrance, and exit, to the room was closely guarded.'

'Nonsense,' snapped the old man rudely. 'What are you trying to tell me? That this murder was committed by someone who had the power to make himself invisible? Rubbish! There's only

112

one solution, and that's obvious to anyone with a grain of sense.'

'I'll be very glad to hear what it is,' said the stout superintendent.

'It's clear enough, isn't it?' growled Mr. Criller. 'There are only two ways of getting into that room and, therefore, the murderer must've used one of 'em.'

'That's impossible, sir,' put in Hawkins. 'Superintendent Budd and I were watching the door, and the two constables were stationed outside the window. No one could have got in either way.'

The old man shrugged his shoulders.

'There is no other way,' he grunted. 'There must have been a time when your guard was not efficient.'

'I'm willing to swear that we never left the window,' interrupted Archer. 'We was there the 'ole time an' never moved a foot, did we, George?'

The other policeman nodded in agreement.

'That's right,' he said heavily. 'No one could've got by us.'

'In any case,' remarked Mr. Budd, stifling a yawn, 'the window was fastened on the inside as I left it. Nobody could've got in that way.'

'Then he must have used the door,' said Mr. Criller stubbornly. 'That's the only possible alternative.'

'That can be ruled out,' said Hawkins. 'I'm prepared to swear that nobody did.'

'In that case, Gottleib must have been killed by a ghost,' sneered the old man, 'an' it'll take a lot to convince me that *that* happened. In my opinion the whole thing was the result of sheer carelessness. I shall have a lot to say about that at the inquest, I can tell you. In the meanwhile, what happens to me? I'm still in danger. This man Seton . . . '

'You still think it was Seton?' asked Mr. Budd, and something in his tone caused the old man to look at him sharply.

'Why not?' he snapped. 'I see no reason why I should change my original opinion. Seton is the only man who ever . . . '

The sudden shrill ringing of the telephone interrupted him. Hawkins turned quickly and hurried into the study. They heard him lift the receiver and speak into the instrument.

'We'll come over at once,' he said. 'Don't touch anything until we arrive.'

Mr. Budd was at the door as the local superintendent came out.

'What was it?' he asked in a low voice.

'Sir Benjamin Gottleib's house has been burgled,' said Hawkins. 'It happened just after midnight. The study was thoroughly ransacked.'

'Did they catch the burglar?' asked Mr. Budd.

Hawkins shook his head.

'No they didn't,' he replied. 'But she was seen.'

'She?' repeated Mr. Budd.

'Yes,' said Hawkins, 'it was a woman.'

★   ★   ★

Helen Longdon fled through the darkness and the rain, her breath panting through her clenched teeth and her heart thumping wildly in her breast. She ran blindly, stumbling over the rough surface of the lane she traversed, and every now and again almost falling as her foot caught in one of the deep ruts.

Her right hand, thrust in the pocket of her blue raincoat, was clutched convulsively round the butt of the tiny automatic which rested there. For the moment she had lost all sense of direction — her one thought was to put as great a distance between herself and the house she had just left as quickly as possible.

She had been seen. She knew that, but she prayed that she had not been recognised.

More by luck than anything else she came out on a secondary road which she knew would take her home. She reached the end of the road and, turning to the left, entered the High Street. No light gleamed in any of the small cottages and shops with which it was lined, and although she peered into every patch of shadow as she passed along there was no living person abroad.

She would have been surprised if there had been. It was nearly one o'clock and the rain had not abated. If anything, it was falling faster than when she had come out, a few minutes after half-past eleven.

She reached the rise of the hill and

began to walk more slowly. At the end was the gate of her house — and sanctuary.

Pausing when she reached the gate, she threw a swift glance round her and slipped into the shadow of the drive. Her feet crunched on the wet gravel as she made her way towards the house. She moved over to one of the grass strips that bordered the path. The thick turf deadened her footsteps, and she proceeded noiselessly, reaching the porch with a sigh of thankfulness.

Groping in the pocket of her raincoat, she found her latchkey, but her hand was shaking so much that it was some time before she could insert the key in the lock of the front door. She had left the big door unbolted, and as the key turned, she felt it open under her pressure.

She was closing the door behind her in the darkness of the hall when the lights suddenly came on.

With a gasp, she turned swiftly.

Jim was standing at the foot of the staircase, his hand still on the switch that controlled the centre pendant.

'Mother!' he exclaimed, and she noticed that his face was pale and glistened with perspiration as though he had been running. 'Where have you been?'

'Don't talk here,' she whispered. 'You'll wake the house.'

'Come into the drawing room,' he said, in such a low voice that she scarcely caught the words. He took her by the arm and led her over to the door on the right of the hall that opened into the big room. He put on the lights and left her while he went to put out those in the hall. When he came back, she was sitting on the arm of a chair near the fireplace, and she noted for the first time that he was fully dressed.

'Where have you been?' he asked as he closed the door.

She passed the tip of her tongue over her dry lips before replying and when she answered she kept her eyes averted.

'I wasn't able to sleep,' she said, and was surprised to find how difficult it was to lie convincingly. 'I thought a walk might do me good . . . '

'Is that the only reason you went out?'

She snatched a quick glance at him and saw that he was watching her intently.

'Of course,' she replied, and succeeded in infusing a note of surprise into her voice. 'What other reason could I have?'

He did not answer at once, but stood fidgeting with a little jade ornament on the mantlepiece.

'Did you go anywhere near Criller's house?' he asked abruptly.

'No, why do you ask that?' she said.

He twisted the little jade image round and round between his finger and thumb.

'Gottleib was killed there — tonight,' he answered.

Her face suddenly became drawn and haggard. She stared up at him with fear-laden eyes.

'How do you know that?' she whispered.

'I couldn't sleep, either,' he said. 'I, too, was out tonight . . . '

It was not a cry she gave, nor a gasp, but a combination of both. Leaving his position by the mantlepiece, he came over and laid his hand gently on his mother's shoulder.

'Why don't you tell me the truth?' he said softly.

Her hand went up and her cold fingers closed tightly round his, but she made no reply.

He waited a moment or two, and then repeated his question.

She raised her head and her lips moved, but no sound came. The hard face looking up into his twitched painfully, the eyes became blurred, and she began to cry, gently at first and then more and more wildly, until he could feel her frail body shaking with the intensity of her sobs . . .

* * *

Doctor Swinley drove Mr. Budd and Hawkins to Sir Benjamin Gottleib's house in his car. They were met by a sleepy-eyed manservant. Hovering in the background of the hall was the partially dressed and agitated figure of a portly man, whom, they presently discovered, was the butler.

A few questions elicited from the

scared servants a rather incoherent story of what had happened.

It was the valet who had first made the discovery. He was a light sleeper, easily disturbed, and shortly after midnight he had wakened and heard the sound of someone moving about in the house below. He knew that his master was not at home, and thinking perhaps that one of the others was ill, he got up, and putting on a dressing gown, came down to see what was the matter.

As he reached the hall he saw that a light was shining through the partially open door of the study. For the first time the possibility that a burglar had broken in occurred to him.

Going softly over to the door, he peered in. The desk lamp was on, and bending over the desk, searching among the papers, was the figure of a woman.

The startled valet moved forward to challenge the intruder, but his foot slipped on the polished floor. He had to cling to the door handle to save himself from falling. The noise he made frightened the woman. She turned and darted through the open French windows leading into the grounds. He recovered himself and went after her, but in the darkness and the rain, he lost her.

Coming back to the house, he roused the butler, and at his suggestion had telephoned to Mr. Criller's house, knowing that his master was spending the night there.

'Did you see this woman's face?' asked Mr. Budd.

The valet shook his head.

'No, sir,' he replied. 'But she was of medium height and dressed in a blue raincoat.'

'You'd better show us the study,' said the stout superintendent, and the valet led them over to the room.

The big centre electrolier was on and in the blaze of light they could see everything distinctly. The drawers of the desk had been forced open and their contents turned out on the broad surface. The French windows were ajar, and a trail of wet footprints, clearly visible on the light carpet, led across to the desk.

'Are these windows usually kept fastened?' asked Mr. Budd, and the butler, who had followed them into the room, nodded.

'Yes, sir. I always fasten all the doors and windows before going to bed.'

The big man went over and looked at the catch.

It had been forced open from the outside. A small bolt which acted as an additional security, had been wrenched from it's fastening and was hanging loose.

The job had been done by an amateur. A professional burglar would have cut out a circle of glass, put in his hand and withdrawn the bolt. It would have been quicker and made less noise. Mr. Budd pushed open the windows and peered out into the wet darkness.

'Which way did the woman go?' he asked.

The valet came over to his side and pointed.

'Across the lawn, sir,' he said. 'I lost her in that patch of shrubbery over there.'

The patch of shrubbery was invisible to Mr. Budd but he gathered that it lay on the other side of the square patch of grass.

Borrowing a torch from the butler, he stepped out on to the broad strip of gravel that ran outside the windows. Directing the light of the torch on this, he was able to make out a double line of footprints that led to the edge of the lawn. Even if the valet had not seen the woman, there could be little doubt of the intruder's sex. The smallness and shape of the heels proved that. They were less clear and easy to follow on the close-cut lawn, but Mr. Budd managed to trace them to a thick belt of laurels that faced the study windows on the opposite side.

Here, he found ample evidence of the woman's progress. Branches had been broken and the soft earth churned up where she had forced her way through the thickly growing bushes.

The shrubbery concealed a low, barbed wire fence which evidently formed one of the boundaries to Gottleib's property. Beyond this, down a steep bank, was a narrow lane, obviously the way that the burglar had made her escape, for on one of the projecting prongs of the wire there hung a little wisp of blue cloth.

It was the material from which raincoats are made and confirmed the description of the woman's apparel.

There were marks on the bank showing where she had slithered down in her hurry to reach the lane; but when the stout superintendent had climbed down laboriously, he discovered that the surface was too rough and unbroken to record any impressions.

Putting the little piece of blue material in his pocket he went back to the house.

Hawkins was questioning the valet, but he broke off as Mr. Budd came in and looked at him inquiringly.

'Find anything?' he asked.

Mr. Budd told him what he had discovered.

'As near as I can gather,' he said, frowning. 'It was twelve-fifteen when this man heard the sound that woke him up. So it's impossible that this woman can have anything to do with the other matter, eh?'

Mr. Budd nodded.

'Apparently,' he remarked. 'Unless she used a car she couldn't have covered the distance between here and Criller's in the time.'

'Which makes it more complicated than ever,' grunted Hawkins, rubbing his chin irritably. 'Who the devil was this woman, and what was she after?'

'It's impossible to tell whether there's anythin' missin',' he said, glancing at the litter on the desk. 'Only Gottleib could tell us that.'

'The master kept nothing of value in his desk, sir,' said the butler a little pompously, for up to now he had been rather relegated to the background. 'All his important documents was kept in the safe.'

'Safe?' said Mr. Budd, looking round the room. 'I don't see any safe . . . '

The butler smiled a superior smile. He crossed to a carved oak cabinet and laid his hand on the top.

'Sir Benjamin had the safe built in 'ere,' he explained. 'He thought it would look less conspicuous.'

Mr. Budd examined the door of the cabinet but it had not been tampered with. It was still locked. He hadn't expected that it would be otherwise. The woman had been disturbed before she had time to do more than glance through the litter on the desk. In any case the safe would probably have proved too much for her to tackle successfully, judging from the way she had broken in.

A search of the papers on the desk revealed that they were, as the butler had said, of little value. There were one or two business letters, dealing with the buying or selling of shares, a quantity of receipted bills, and that was all.

There was little more they could do here, and after telling the horrified butler of the death of his master, they went back to Mr. Criller's house.

To Mr. Budd's intense annoyance they had to walk, for Doctor Swinley had only dropped them on the way to his own house. He grumbled all the way under his breath about this unwonted exercise.

When they eventually arrived, they found that the old man had roused Grace and the servants. He and the girl, in company with Percy and the three policemen, were drinking coffee in the drawing room, and Hawkins and Mr. Budd gratefully accepted their invitation to join them. They were chilled to the bone from their walk in the icy rain.

Mr. Criller was intensely curious to know what had happened and poured forth a string of questions which they answered as shortly as possible.

'I don't understand it,' he declared, his yellow face puckered into a grimace of perplexity. 'I don't understand it at all. There's something devilish going on, and I don't mind admitting that I'm scared. I rely on you to see that no harm comes to me. You understand? I *insist* that I'm guarded with the utmost care.'

Hawkins tried to reassure the old man, but the murder of Gottleib had shaken his faith in the infallibility of the police.

They stayed until the ambulance had been and taken the body away, and then, leaving Archer and Bridges on guard, with strict instructions, backed up by Mr. Criller, not to leave the old man out of their sight, they took their departure.

Mr. Budd was tired, worried, and not a little irritable. He accompanied the local superintendent as far as the police station, and then, with a promise that he would look in first thing in the morning, went back to the inn.

He undressed and got into bed at once, but it was a long time before he got to sleep. His mind kept going over every detail of the incredible crime which had been committed almost in front of his eyes.

And the more he thought about it, the more impossible it seemed.

The window of his bedroom had turned from black to grey, before he finally dropped off into an uneasy sleep . . .

★ ★ ★

Mr. Whipper was brought up before an unsympathetic magistrate who was not disposed to listen to his passionate plea of police persecution. He interrupted Mr. Whipper's pathetic oration, and briefly committed him for trial.

The little burglar shrugged his shoulders philosophically, and leaving the dock, was conducted by a good-natured constable to the waiting car which was to take him back to his cell.

During the journey he became loquacious.

'I don't really bear no malice,' he said virtuously. 'It's your job to pinch as many people durin' the year as you can. You must make mistakes now an' again. I don't s'pose you often make such a bloomer as pinchin' a chap as innercent as me . . . '

'What's the good of bluffin', Whipper?' said his guardian good-humouredly. 'You was caught good an' proper, with the stuff on you, so why make a song an' dance about it?'

Mr. Whipper capitulated.

'Well, I suppose they'll believe the police before they'll believe me,' he said. 'But 'ow those jewel cases got in my pocket is a mystery to me.'

'I'll bet it is,' said the sergeant. 'It's always a mystery to you fellers how the goods gets on you. Almost as big a mystery as this murder what 'appened last night.'

Mr. Whipper pricked up his ears and his eyes gleamed with interest.

'What murder's that?' he asked quickly.

The sergeant, who was prone to gossip, told him. A curious expression came into the face of the little burglar as he listened.

'What was the feller's name?' he asked. 'The feller what was killed?'

'Sir Benjamin Gottleib,' said the sergeant importantly. 'Nearly a millionaire, 'e was, from all accounts. It's the second murder what's 'appened round here during the last few days. Both at this feller, Criller's house, too. The other chap was a friend of his called Franklin Brinn . . .'

'Franklin Brinn!' Mr. Whipper sat bolt upright.

''Ere, are you sure o' that?'

'Of course, I'm sure,' answered the surprised sergeant. 'Why?'

'Never you mind 'why',' said the little burglar excitedly. 'Who's in charge of this case?'

'Superintendent Hawkins an' Superintendent Budd,' said the sergeant.

'Budd, eh?' said Mr. Whipper. ''E's in

131

it, is he? Look 'ere, as soon as we get back to the police station you put a call through to Budd an' tell 'im to come along an' see me . . . '

'What's the idea?' asked the surprised sergeant suspiciously.

'Never you mind,' said Mr. Whipper. 'I ain't discussin' it with you, anyway.'

He shut up like an oyster, and all the sergeant's cajoling failed to elicit anything further.

When they reached the station, Mr. Whipper's request was made known to the inspector, and after a great deal of hesitation, for the little burglar refused to give his reason for wishing to get in touch with the Scotland Yard man, the call was put through.

Mr. Budd was sitting in Hawkins's office when the message arrived, and he frowned when he heard who it was who wished to speak to him.

'Whipper?' he muttered. 'Yes, I know him. What does he want?'

The desk sergeant shook his grizzled head.

'He won't say,' he answered. 'He says 'e

won't tell anybody but you, sir.'

Mr. Budd rose wearily, went out into the charge room, and picked up the receiver.

'Hello,' he called. 'Is that you, Whipper?'

'Is that Sup'n'tendent Budd?' came the high-pitched voice of the little burglar. 'Listen, Sooper, can you come over ter my 'otel? It ain't very comfortable, an' the staff's rotten, but I've got somethin' ter tell you . . . '

'Now, you know, I can't do anythin' for you,' began Mr. Budd.

'But I can do somethin' for *you*,' interrupted Mr. Whipper. 'You're workin' on these murders — Brinn an' the other feller, ain't yer?'

Mr. Budd's expression changed.

'What do you know about 'em?' he asked quickly.

'You come over 'ere, an' I'll tell yer,' said Mr. Whipper. 'I can't tell you on the blower — there's no privacy in this place. All the flat-footed coppers in the station are listening.'

The stout superintendent smiled.

'All right,' he said, 'I'll come at once.'

'Stay to lunch,' said the irrepressible Mr. Whipper. 'I'll reserve a table in the grill-room!'

Mr. Budd hung up the receiver and went back to Hawkins. That individual listened as he briefly explained the gist of Mr. Whipper's message.

'What can he know?' he said, scratching his chin.

'Maybe nothin',' answered Mr. Budd, 'but on the other hand, maybe a lot.'

'I'll be interested to hear if he can explain how Gottleib came to be shot in that locked room and what happened to the murderer,' grunted Hawkins. 'That'd be worth hearing!'

It took Mr. Budd twenty minutes to reach the police station in which the unfortunate Mr. Whipper was incarcerated, and after a brief word with the inspector, he was conducted to the cell.

The little burglar was reclining at his ease on the pallet bed, but he sat up as the stout superintendent entered, and greeted him with a grin.

'Sit down, Sooper,' he said airily. 'I

s'pose you don't 'appen to 'ave a fag on yer?'

'I never smoke 'em,' said Mr. Budd, shaking his head. 'I can give you a cigar . . . '

'Not one of them things *you* smoke,' said Mr. Whipper with a grimace. 'Cor lumme, the smell of 'em's enough to kill an 'orse! I 'ad some fags on me,' he continued libellously, 'but one of the flatties pinched 'em when I was searched.'

'You had nothing on you except half a crown,' broke in the inspector sternly.

'An' where is it?' demanded Mr. Whipper. 'Gone ter the funds o' the police orphanage, I suppose?'

'It wouldn't help 'em much, if it had,' growled the inspector. 'It was 'snide'.'

'Now then,' said Mr. Budd. 'What was it you wanted to see me about, eh? I can't stop here all day, you know.'

'I ain't talkin' before 'im,' said Mr. Whipper, jerking his head towards the inspector. 'What I've got ter say is private.'

The inspector, who was used to the ways of Mr. Whipper's kind, looked at

Mr. Budd and smiled.

'I suppose I'd better leave you together,' he said genially.

'An' don't forget the lunch,' said the burglar. 'I want the best the 'ouse can provide an' a table overlookin' Green Park!'

'We don't do lunches at this hotel,' retorted the inspector. 'You'll have to wait until you're moved to Pentonville!'

He left them with a chuckle.

'If there's a law in the land, that feller oughter get 'ung one of these days,' said Mr. Whipper darkly.

'There isn't, you've broken 'em all,' said Mr. Budd. 'Now, what do you know about these murders, eh?'

The little burglar looked at him for several seconds in silence.

'You know what I'm 'ere for, don't yer?' he said at last, and Mr. Budd nodded. 'Well, between you an' me, it was a fair cop, though I wouldn't say that to everyone. But you're a chap what can respect a feller's confidence.'

'There's a difference between respectin' a confidence an' compoundin' a felony,' Mr. Budd pointed out.

'All right, it don't make no difference,' said Mr. Whipper. 'They've got me, any'ow. An' you can bet your sweet life they'll keep me. Whether you keep what I'm goin' to tell yer to yerself or spread it around. See? It won't make no difference. If I'd 'ad any luck, I'd've got clean away. But I didn't 'ave no luck, an' that's all there is to it.' He shrugged his shoulders. 'What I wanted ter tell yer is this; while I was up in that bedroom 'avin' a squint round, I found a little book. It was lyin' on the dressin' table. Only a little thing — about so big.' He indicated with his hands an object the size of a pocket diary. 'Bein' of a curious disposition, I looked ter see what was in it. There wasn't much, mostly appointments an' figures. But on one page there was three names. They didn't mean nothin' ter me at the time, but when that big-footed sergeant told me about the murders, I remembered . . . '

'What were the names?' asked Mr. Budd, as he paused.

'Brinn, Gottleib, an' Criller,' answered

Mr. Whipper impressively. 'But that ain't all.' He leaned forward and pointed his words with stabs of his finger. 'Underneath was written the words: 'My 'usband's murderers.''

7

Superintendent Hawkins was talking to a dapper man with a fattish, florid face, when Mr. Budd got back from his interview with Mr. Whipper. He introduced the red-faced man as Major Candy, the Chief Constable for the County.

'How d'ye do,' said the Major, in a deep, rather hoarse voice that, coming from a man of such a small stature, was a little startling. 'This is an extraordinary business, eh? Deuced extraordinary.'

Mr. Budd thoroughly agreed with him and said so.

'Very glad you were on the spot,' went on the Major. Hawkins has just given me all the details, and I'm hanged if I can see how it could've happened.'

'No more can I, sir, at the moment,' said Mr. Budd. 'But there must be an explanation . . . '

'Must be a secret entrance to the room,' declared the Chief Constable.

'If there is, it's the finest secret I've ever come up against,' said the big man. 'We've examined that room so well that we know every fly mark.'

'I'd be willing to swear there isn't a secret entrance, sir,' said Hawkins.

'The thing's incredible,' grunted Major Candy. 'You've been over to see this man, Whipper, I'm told?'

'Yes, sir,' replied Mr. Budd. He told them what the little burglar had had to say, and Hawkins frowned.

'Do you think he was speaking the truth?' he asked. 'Maybe, he's just making it up to be sensational.'

'He was speakin' the truth,' said Mr. Budd. 'I can generally tell when these fellers are lyin', an' Whipper wasn't.'

'But the Longdons,' protested the Chief Constable, pursing his lips. 'I know them very well. Mrs. Longdon's a charming woman. Charming! I don't think she even knew Gottleib, and I'm certain she didn't know Brinn . . . '

'Her son knows Miss Hatton,' remarked Mr. Budd. 'It was his handkerchief that we found at the beginnin' of the path that

140

leads down to the summerhouse where Brinn was killed.'

'Yes, that's right,' exclaimed Hawkins.

'I wasn't altogether satisfied with Miss Hatton's explanation of how it got there,' went on the stout man.

'But the Longdons,' muttered the Major again, pinching his chin and frowning. 'It's absurd to suppose that they could have anything to do with these murders . . . '

'Why is it?' asked Mr. Budd, looking at him sleepily. 'Apart from the fact that you consider Mrs. Longdon a charmin' woman, what do you know about 'em, sir?'

The Chief Constable's eyebrows shot up in surprise. For a moment he was silent and then he said:

'Well, if you put it like that, nothing,' he admitted rather lamely.

'Did you ever meet the husband?' asked Mr. Budd.

The Major shook his head.

'No. I believe he died several years ago,' he answered. 'Mrs. Longdon was a widow when she first came here.'

141

'How long ago is that?'

The Chief Constable considered.

'Eight years — may be a little longer,' he replied. 'The house had been empty for some time when she took it and moved in with her son.'

'Was Criller livin' here then?' asked Mr. Budd, and the Major nodded.

'Yes, he'd been here — let me see — about ten years,' he answered.

'And Gottleib?'

'He didn't come until much later,' said the Major. 'About five years ago . . . '

Mr. Budd stroked the lowest of his many chins gently.

'It wouldn't do any harm if we knew a bit more about these Longdons,' he said. 'Where they came from . . . I'm goin' up to London this afternoon, and I'll have a few inquiries made.'

He left the Chief Constable and Hawkins to discuss the arrangements for the double inquest, had a light lunch, got out his car, and set off on his journey to London.

He arrived in the middle of the afternoon and drove straight to Scotland

142

Yard. When he was seated in his bare office, he sent for Sergeant Leek.

That melancholy man came ambling into the office.

'What were you doin'?' asked Mr. Budd. 'Havin' a sleep, I'll bet?'

'I was in the canteen,' answered the sergeant. ''Avin' a cup o' tea. I didn't expect you . . . '

'Well, I'm here,' said Mr. Budd, 'An' I've got a lot ter tell you. So try an' keep awake long enough to listen.'

He gave a brief account of the murders. The thin-faced Leek listened with interest.

'Sounds like one of these 'ere thrillers,' he remarked. 'Thin's like that don't 'appen in real life.'

'Well, this has,' snapped his superior. 'I'm not makin' it up to amuse you! I'm hopin' that you'll have some intelligent suggestions to make.'

He lit one of his objectionable cigars and leaned back in his chair. The long face of Leek lengthened, and he shifted uncomfortably from one foot to another. Here was an opportunity to show his brilliance, but he couldn't think of anything.

Mr. Budd watched him through half-closed eyes while he trickled smoke through his nostrils.

'Stop dancin' about an' sit down,' he said irritably. 'What d'you think you're doin'? Practisin' for the Russian Ballet, eh?'

Leek sat down.

The expression of concentration on his face was frightful.

'Stop makin' faces,' said Mr. Budd. 'It's bad enough when you leave it alone.'

'I can't suggest anythin',' muttered the miserable Leek after several minutes. 'You an' Hawkins was watchin' the door an' the two policemen was outside the winder. I can't see . . . ' He stopped abruptly and his watery eyes widened suddenly.

'Go on,' said Mr. Budd encouragingly. 'Impossible as it may seem, I believe you've had an idea.'

'I was only wonderin',' ventured Leek hesitantly, 'if those two policemen was outside the winder . . . '

The cigar which the stout man had been raising to his lips came to a stop in mid-air.

'They both swear they never moved,' he said thoughtfully.

'That's not to say they didn't,' pointed out Leek 'It was a nasty night, wasn't it? Cold an' wet. They may've got a bit chilly an' taken a turn or two to warm themselves. They wouldn't admit it in the circumstances, would they?'

Mr. Budd took a long pull at his cigar.

'It's incredible that you could say anythin' intelligent,' he said at last, 'but I believe you 'ave this time. It's worth lookin' into.' He got heavily to his feet.

'I'm goin' along to see Weaver,' he announced. 'See if you can get any more brain waves.'

He left the gratified sergeant, and lumbered out of the office. Inspector Weaver was sitting at his desk reading through a long report when Mr. Budd came in.

Without preliminary, the stout man explained the reason for his visit. The dark-featured Weaver listened with an expressionless face.

'It seems to me that you've got a pretty pill in front of you,' he said, when Mr. Budd had finished. 'Of course, you realise that even if you knew the person who shot Gottleib, until you can prove how he got in and out of that room, no jury would convict, eh?'

'I know that,' said Mr. Budd. 'What I want you to do, is look up these Longdons. I want to know all about 'em, an' I want to know soon. I also want to know anythin' you can find out about Criller, Gottleib, and Brinn. You might also tell me all that's known about a feller named Seton . . . '

'Anything else?' asked Weaver sarcastically.

'That'll do to be goin' on with,' said Mr. Budd.

'I can tell you something off hand,' said Weaver. 'Brinn was a pretty bad hat . . . '

'That's interestin'. In what way?'

'All sorts of ways,' answered Weaver. 'We've had our eyes on Franklin Brinn for a long time. When I heard he'd been murdered, I can't say I was surprised.

Mind you, we've never had enough on him to take any action. He was just one of those people who were under suspicion. You know what a lot of 'em there are? He never did anything that we could have got him for, but he sailed very close to the wind.'

'He was a broker, wasn't he?' murmured Mr. Budd.

Weaver nodded.

'He had a little office in Mooregate Street, but he was interested in anything that offered a chance of putting money in his pocket. But, as I say, we could never pin anything on him.'

'Well, that's interestin',' said Mr. Budd. 'It don't help very much at the moment, though. Have you ever heard anythin' about this feller, Seton?'

'No, but I'll try an' trace him up for you,' said Weaver.

'Trace everybody up,' said Mr. Budd. 'I'd like to know everythin' that's possible about everybody connected with this case.'

'Right you are,' said Weaver cheerfully. 'I'll do my best.'

Mr Budd returned to his office with the pleasant feeling that he had done all he could — or so he thought then. Three days later he realised that there was one important detail that had been overlooked, but by the time he became aware of it, it no longer mattered.

★   ★   ★

Mr. Criller was in his very worst mood. Throughout the day he snapped and snarled at everybody who came in contact with him, and since this had been mostly Grace, she had suffered more than her share of his irritability.

On Mr. Budd's instructions the study had been sealed. Every member of the household had been warned that on no account were the seals to be broken or the room entered.

This had exasperated the old man to a state of fury.

'Am I to be inconvenienced, and possibly lose a great deal of money,' he cried, stamping up and down the long drawing room, 'because the police are so incompetent that they allow a man to be killed under their very eyes? Bah! It's sickening! I had a lot of work to do today which necessitates my having access to my files. Now I've got to wait until a lot of bone-headed policemen allow me to enter my own study!'

He raved and cursed for over an hour, and Grace, who was used to these outbursts, listened in silence.

In these moods, Mr. Criller was impossible. To argue with him would have made matters worse, and to agree with him would have brought forth a stream of vituperation. So she took refuge in silence.

She would have given a great deal to have left him and gone to snatch a few hours of the rest she so badly needed. But she was afraid that any suggestion of the sort would act like a match to a barrel of gunpowder. Her prison had been bad enough before, but now it was almost unendurable, for into the atmosphere of the house had crept a kind of stealthy terror that caused her heart to jump at the slightest unaccustomed sound, and made her fearful of every shadowy corner and dread the coming of night.

After a while, without a word, Mr. Criller left the drawing room, and she heard him go up the stairs and lock himself in his bedroom.

She felt a certain amount of relief when she was alone. The removal of the dominating personality of the old man left her free to think, and her thoughts turned to Jim Longdon.

She had only seen him for a few minutes since she had made the horrible discovery in the summerhouse. At that brief meeting there had not been the time to say the things she wanted to say. She wanted to ask him about the handker-chief . . .

Although she could not bring herself to believe that Jim had anything to do with the affair, the finding of the handkerchief had given her a shock.

How had it got there?

She had puzzled over this for a long time without finding any satisfactory answer. Of course, he must have dropped it, but to her knowledge he had never been near that part of the garden. Another thing, too, which made her uneasy was the memory of certain questions which he had put to her during their brief meetings. He had shown more than a normal interest in Mr. Criller and his affairs; had wanted to know about his friends and what he did for a living.

She had been rather surprised at the time, but had put it down to mere idle curiosity. Now these questions came back to her with an added significance.

Had he had some obscure reason for asking them? A reason that was connected with the double tragedy that had burst upon them so suddenly?

His mother, too, on the only occasion when she had met her, had expressed an inordinate curiosity concerning the old man. She tried to thrust these thoughts away from her. Somehow they seemed a little disloyal. But they kept on recurring, in spite of her efforts, and each time the slight suspicion that lurked in her heart grew stronger.

She refused to admit it, even to herself, but it was there.

Lunch was served punctually as usual. Mr. Criller came down and took his place at the head of the table. Throughout the meal, he spoke not a single word, keeping his eyes fixed on his plate.

But once. Grace looked up unexpectedly and saw that he was watching her intently. She was glad when the meal ended. To her relief he went back to his room, and, seeking her own, she lay down on the bed and was asleep almost at once.

It was four o'clock when she awoke, washed, tidied her hair and came downstairs.

The housemaid was in the hall, and she learned that Mr. Criller had given orders that tea was to be brought to him in his room, and that he was not to be disturbed until dinner-time.

She had her own tea in the drawing-room, and then, obeying a sudden impulse to get out of the house into fresh air, she put on her coat and went out.

The air was damp and cold, but it smelt clean and fresh. The wonderful scent of wet earth filled her nostrils as she walked down the winding path to the little gate. She hesitated for a moment when she reached the lane, wondering which way to take. She decided that it would be better to avoid the village, and turned in the direction of the open country.

It seemed to her that with her exit from the house a great weight had been lifted from her shoulders. It was a relief not to hear the querulous voice of Mr. Criller alternately complaining and bullying. There was also another reason which she was honest enough to admit to herself. The way which she had chosen was one of Jim's favourite walks, and there was a possibility that she might meet him.

She was half way through the wood when she saw the figure of a man approaching, and her heart gave a jump. But as she drew closer, she saw that it was not the person she hoped it might be.

The man was Percy Gottleib.

She had no desire to talk to him, and contemplated leaving the narrow path and plunging in among the trees. But he had already seen her. It was too late to do anything except continue on her way.

His sallow face contorted into a pleased leer as they met.

'Hello, Miss Hatton,' he greeted. 'This is a pleasant surprise. As a matter of fact I was just coming along to see Criller.'

'You'll find him at home,' she said, hoping that he would take the hint, but Percy Gottleib was impervious to hints, broad or otherwise.

'There's no particular hurry,' he said. 'It's nothing very important. Where are you going?'

His unpleasant little eyes searched her face, and there was a greedy look in them which she found rather embarrassing.

'For a walk,' she answered shortly, and would have passed him, but he turned and fell in at her side.

'I'll come with you,' he said. 'I haven't been out all day.'

She bit her lip in vexation. She had no wish for the weedy youth's company but, since she could not say so without being unnecessarily rude, she had to make the best of it.

For a moment they walked on in silence, Percy giving her approving glances out of the corner of his eye.

'How's the old man?' he asked presently.

'Do you mean Mr. Criller?' she said, and when he nodded: 'He's very upset, naturally.'

She was deliberately non-communicative, hoping that he would sense her dislike of his society. But Percy's hide was thick, and, even if he noticed her lack of cordiality, he gave no sign.

'I'll bet he's upset,' he remarked with a chuckle. 'And I'll bet he's going to be more upset before he's much older.'

It was on the tip of her tongue to ask him what he meant, but she thought better of it and made no comment.

'He gives you a pretty rough time, doesn't he?' he went on, and when she did not answer: 'I don't know why you stick it. A pretty girl like you could have a good time, if she wanted to. Why do you stay here at the beck and call of that old devil?'

A latent sense of loyalty forced her to take up the cudgels on the old man's behalf.

'He's been very good to me,' she said.

'Good to you!' Percy snorted contemptuously. 'Why, he treats you like a slave. You never go anywhere or do anything. It's a rotten life for a girl! What you want is some excitement. Theatres, dances. What about coming up to Town with me one of these nights, eh?'

'Thank you,' she said, 'but I'd rather not.'

'Oh, don't talk rot!' he answered rudely. 'If you're thinking of old Criller, I'll soon fix him.'

'I wasn't thinking of Mr. Criller,' she replied quietly. 'I just don't want to go out with you, that's all.'

'I don't see why you have to be so confoundedly stand-offish,' he grumbled. 'I like you, Grace. We could be good friends you and me. I'll have money now, you know. I can give a girl a good time . . . '

'I think I'll go back home now,' she interrupted, but he caught her arm.

'You don't want to go yet,' he said. 'Look here, why can't we fix up an evening together, eh? Just say where you'd

156

like to go and I'll fix it up . . . '

'It's very kind of you,' she said, 'but I'd rather not. Would you mind letting go of my arm?'

He stared at her, and then, before she realised his intention, he drew her quickly towards him and kissed her on the lips.

'There,' he said, as she struggled away from him. 'That's on account of many others, I hope.'

With a flaming face and smouldering eyes she faced him.

'You nasty little cad,' she said, and her voice was like the flick of a whiplash. 'How dared you do that?'

Percy's pasty face went mottled — ugly patches of red that stood out against his unhealthy pallor.

'Why go on like the heroine in a melodrama?' he sneered. 'I don't suppose it's the first time a man's kissed you, and I'm damned sure it won't be the last . . . '

'It'll be the last as far as you're concerned!' snapped an angry voice, and they both turned to find Jim Longdon standing within a few feet of them. He had been rambling about in the wood and had come upon them without either having heard his approach.

'You mind your own business,' snarled Percy, his eyes snapping dangerously.

'It is my business,' retorted Jim.

An unpleasant look crossed the other's face and his lips curled back from his teeth.

'Poaching on your preserves, eh?' he said. 'I see. So that's why you wouldn't come out with me, is it?' He leered at the girl. 'Other fish to fry. I thought you weren't so shy and innocent as you tried to make out . . . '

He stopped with a yelp of pain as Jim's bunched fist shot out and hit him on that sneering mouth. Percy staggered back and fell amongst the decayed bracken at the side of the little footpath.

'I'll get back on you for that,' he mumbled. 'I'll get back on both of you! You just watch out . . . '

Without even looking at him, Jim Longdon took the girl by the arm.

'Come along,' he said authoritatively. 'We'll leave that crawling thing among the other crawling things in the bracken.'

She went with him, pale-faced and a little frightened.

Percy got slowly to his feet and wiped his cut lips with his handkerchief. The expression on his face was not pleasant as he glared after them.

'Just you wait,' he muttered venomously. 'Just you wait. I know a lot more than you think — a lot more . . . '

★　★　★

Mr. Budd came back to the little creeper-covered inn in the village during the early part of that afternoon.

When he had had some tea and a wash, he went down to the police station to find Hawkins.

The superintendent was working at his desk in the small office, but he pushed the papers aside when the big man came in.

'Glad to see you back,' he greeted. 'We've fixed the inquest for ten o'clock tomorrow morning. It'll be a very formal affair, of course. I've seen the coroner, and except for the medical evidence and

159

the evidence of identification, no witnesses will be called, and we shall ask for a fortnight's adjournment.'

Mr. Budd nodded.

'That's the best thing,' he agreed.

'How did you get on?' asked Hawkins.

The stout man shrugged his shoulders.

'I've set a whole lot o' wheels turnin',' he answered, 'an' we may have some results. My sergeant, rather surprisin'ly offered a suggestion that might be worth lookin' into.'

He told Hawkins what Leek had said concerning the two policemen.

The superintendent frowned and pursed his lips.

'I think they would have told us if they'd moved away from the window,' he remarked. 'Still, there's no harm in asking them. They're on duty up at Criller's now, but as soon as they come back, I'll have 'em in and question them.'

'I suppose you haven't discovered anythin' fresh?' asked Mr. Budd.

Hawkins gave vent to a little snort of disgust.

'Not a thing,' he declared. 'Gottleib's

lawyer's coming down this afternoon.'

'Maybe, he can tell us somethin',' said Mr. Budd.

'It's about time somebody did,' replied Hawkins despondently. 'It's getting me down.'

'It's the 'how' that worries me,' said the stout man. 'How could anyone have killed Gottleib in the circumstances?'

'I don't know,' said the local man, shaking his head. 'But it was managed somehow. There's no doubt that he was shot in that room.'

Mr. Budd stared at the window in silence.

'What time is this lawyer feller arrivin'?' he asked after a pause.

'His train's due at five o'clock,' answered Hawkins. 'They're sending a car to meet him at the station. It'll take about five minutes to reach the house, so he ought to be there at five-fifteen. Why?'

'I'd like to have a word with him,' remarked Mr. Budd, yawning.

Hawkins looked at his watch.

'If we walk up to the house,' he said, 'we ought to get there just about the same

161

time as he does.'

Mr. Budd, who loathed walking at any time, looked a little dubious at this suggestion, but he reluctantly agreed.

'All right,' he said. 'Let's go.'

Hawkins got up from the desk, struggled into his overcoat, put on his hat, and, after a word to the sergeant in charge, left the station-house, and set off up the hill to Gottleib's house.

Just as they reached the gates of the drive, a car came swinging round the bend in the road and they had to step aside to avoid it. It was a big Rolls and Hawkins nudged Mr. Budd's arm.

'That's the car,' he said. 'We've judged the time pretty well.'

The big machine swung into the drive and they followed it on foot. By the time they reached the front door, the car had discharged its burden and was standing, empty, in front of the steps, with a neatly uniformed chauffeur standing beside it.

Followed by the panting Mr. Budd, who was breathless from his unusual exercise, Hawkins ascended the steps and rang the bell.

The butler admitted them, and asked them to wait in the hall while he vanished in the direction of the study.

There was some delay before he returned and asked them to follow him into the big room.

The weedy figure of Percy Gottleib was sitting at the desk, and before him, perched on one of the leather chairs, was one of the smallest men Mr. Budd had ever seen. He must have been under five feet in height when he was standing up, and his thinness was almost painful to look at.

On his knees was an open briefcase which appeared to be bulging with documents, one of which the lawyer had been on the point of withdrawing at their entrance, for it was half in and half out, one end still grasped in his skinny hand.

The pasty-faced Percy greeted them curtly.

'I don't know what you want,' he said, 'but I'm very busy at the moment. This is Mr. Scruten, my late father's solicitor.'

The thin man gave an almost imperceptible little nod to signify that he had heard the introduction; gave them both a shrewd glance from narrowed, slit-like eyes, and then looked down again at his papers.

'Sorry to disturb you,' said Mr. Budd smoothly, 'but knowin' that your lawyer was comin' here today, we took the opportunity of callin' so that we could ask him one or two questions.'

Mr. Scruten looked up sharply. The stout man was under the impression that he was going to say something, but the tight, lipless mouth remained closed.

'Well, I suppose there's no harm in that,' grunted Percy ungraciously. 'Still, you might have given me a chance to have a word with him myself first. You'd better carry on. We can go into my business later.'

Mr. Budd thanked him and turned to the little man.

'The thing we're interested in,' he said, in his slow and ponderous way, 'is the late Sir Benjamin's will . . .'

'That's what I'm interested in, too,' interposed Percy.

'I presume,' went on Mr. Budd, taking

no notice of the interruption, 'that his foster-son inherits the property?'

The almost invisible mouth of Mr. Scruten opened and from somewhere in his small, skinny body came a most unexpected voice, a deep, growling bass that was so completely out of keeping with his general appearance, that Hawkins almost gaped in his surprise.

'I entirely fail, sir,' he said, 'to understand on what grounds you base such an assumption.'

Percy looked at him quickly, and the cigarette he had been raising to his lips dropped from his fingers on to the blotting-pad.

'What do you mean by that, Scruten?' he demanded shrilly. 'You're not telling me that the old man didn't . . . ?'

He stopped as the lawyer held up one of his bony hands.

'Please,' he boomed. 'Please! Before these gentlemen came in I was about to make you acquainted with the contents of your foster-father's will. If it is your wish that I should do so in their presence, I will proceed.'

Percy picked up the cigarette which was burning a brown hole in the blotting-pad, hesitated for a moment, and then nodded.

'Carry on,' he said. 'I don't see why there should be anything secret about it.'

Mr. Scruten completely withdrew the document he had been holding, out of the briefcase, unfolded it carefully, cleared his throat, and began to read:

' "This is the last will and testament of me, Benj . . . " '

'Oh, skip all that,' broke in Percy impatiently. 'Who gets the boodle? That's all I want to know. I don't understand all that legal stuff.'

Mr. Scruten looked a trifle disgruntled. 'It's rather irregular,' he began.

'Never mind whether it's irregular or not,' snapped Percy. 'Get down to brass tacks. Who gets the money?'

It seemed to the watchful Mr. Budd that he was a little anxious. There was a strained look in his small eyes, and the hand that held the half-smoked cigarette shook slightly.

Mr. Scruten coughed.

'Well, then, briefly,' he said, glancing at the document in his hand, 'you receive this house, with an income of two thousand a year during your lifetime. The residue of the estate is to be divided equally between George Hammond and Cecil Purvis.'

'What's that?' The ejaculation came from Percy, huskily and chokily. His pasty face grew even paler and then changed to an angry red. 'What's that? Tell me again.'

The solicitor obligingly complied.

'Two thousand a year for life,' muttered Percy. 'Why that's nothing! The mean old devil! The dirty double-crossing old hound!'

He almost choked with the rage that was consuming him.

'Really,' said Mr. Scruten admonishingly. 'I must protest against your language . . .'

'To hell with my language!' stormed Percy, beside himself with rage. 'Wouldn't you be annoyed if you'd been treated like I have? Who are these people, Hammond and Purvis?'

Mr. Scruten shook his egg-shaped head.

'I'm afraid I can't tell you that,' he replied. 'I don't know.'

'Does that mean you've never met 'em?' asked Mr. Budd, before the outraged Percy could open his mouth again.

'It means exactly what I said, sir,' answered the lawyer. 'I have never met these people, nor have I ever heard of them before . . .'

'Didn't you draw up the will?' demanded Percy.

Again the little lawyer shook his head.

'No,' he replied. 'The will was drawn up by Sir Benjamin himself. It was deposited with me in a sealed envelope with instructions that it was only to be opened in the event of his death.'

Mr. Budd frowned and scratched all his chins.

Here was a fresh mystery.

'When was this will deposited with you?' he asked.

'Ten years ago,' answered Mr. Scruten. 'There is a further clause which states that should either of the two men named pre-decease Sir Benjamin, then the entire residue of the estate shall go to the survivor. Should they both pre-decease him, then Mr. Percy Gottleib here' — he nodded towards the savage Percy — 'receives the lot.'

'Well, that's something,' growled that gentleman. 'Perhaps these two fellows are dead, eh?'

'I haven't the least idea,' said Mr. Scruten. 'Neither have I any idea where they are to be found.'

'Aren't their addresses in the will?' asked Superintendent Hawkins.

'No,' answered Mr. Scruten. 'That struck me as rather peculiar. There is, you see, no means of acquainting them of their good fortune.'

'Good thing, too,' grunted Percy. 'Well, if they're alive and put in a claim, I shall contest it.'

'You would be very ill-advised to do so,' said the lawyer curtly. 'Providing these men prove their identity they are entitled to an equal share in the residue of the estate. There isn't a court in the country that wouldn't uphold them.'

'It's a dirty trick,' burst out Percy. 'The

old man always gave me to understand that I should come into his money. What's the good of leaving me a mouldy two thousand a year?'

'You get the house as well,' pointed out the solicitor.

'A fat lot of good that is,' grumbled Percy. 'If I live in it, it'll cost half my income to keep it up. If I sell it what would I get for it? Precious little, I'll bet.'

Mr. Scruten made no reply. Patently he was not very much interested in Percy Gottleib's affairs.

'Didn't your foster-father ever mention either of these names to you?' asked Mr. Budd.

Percy shook his head angrily.

'Never heard of 'em before in my life,' he snarled. 'The old man must have been mad when he made that will. George Hammond and Cecil Purvis! Bah! Who are they, and what are they?'

Nobody answered him because nobody could.

Mr. George Hammond and Mr. Cecil Purvis were names, and nothing more. They had neither shape nor substance.

But, supposing them to be still alive, they had, or would have, a very large amount of money.

Mr. Budd pinched his lower lip and stared dreamily at the ceiling.

Was this the motive behind the death of Gottleib? If so, what connection had it with the murder of Franklin Brinn and the threat against the yellow-faced Mr. Criller?

8

Mr. Budd slowly consumed the final portion of the excellent piece of Stilton which had rounded off his dinner, and got up from the table. Ordering coffee to be sent up to his room, he mounted, with some little difficulty, the narrow staircase of the old-fashioned inn in which he was staying, and prepared for an evening of quiet, concentrated thought.

He switched on the light, and when the coffee arrived, carried it over to the small table beside the bed. Taking off his jacket he pulled on a dressing gown, loosened his collar, lit one of his unpleasant cigars, and proceeded to make himself comfortable on the bed.

He was just beginning to marshal his thoughts when there came a tap at the door.

In reply to his rather irritable invitation, the rosy-cheeked girl, who combined waitress and general help at the inn, entered.

'If you please, sir,' she said, 'there's a gentleman asking for you.'

Mr. Budd frowned at the glowing end of the cigar between his stubby fingers.

'Who is it?' he growled.

'Mr. Percy Gottleib,' answered the girl. 'He's waiting downstairs in the parlour. Shall I ask him to come up?'

The stout man considered for a moment and then shook his head.

'I'll come down,' he said. 'Tell him I won't be a minute.'

The girl departed, and hoisting himself laboriously off the bed, Mr. Budd stripped off the dressing gown, adjusted his collar and tie, resumed his jacket, and went downstairs, wondering what this unexpected visit from the weedy Percy portended.

He found that unpleasant youth scowling at one of the old-fashioned pictures on the wall of the small parlour. He turned round as Mr. Budd entered and greeted him with an uneasy grin.

'Sorry to disturb you,' he began with

unusual politeness, 'but I wanted to . . . '

He stopped suddenly and his expression changed. The intended-to-be-pleasant smile vanished and was replaced by a cunning look. However Percy had intended to end that sentence originally, he had changed his mind. Quite suddenly and abruptly. Some thought had struck him even while the words were hovering on the tip of his tongue. This was so blatantly evident that he might as well have said so in so many words.

'There's no need to apologise,' said Mr. Budd, pretending to have noticed nothing. 'Why do you wish to see me?'

Percy Gottleib passed the tip of his tongue over his lips. A light of excitement had crept into his small, pig-like eyes.

'It was about this — this ridiculous will,' he stammered. 'Scruten says that it would be useless to contest it, but I was wondering, perhaps, since you've had experience in this sort of thing, that you might be able to advise me?'

The words were jerky, uttered without any thought behind them. Mr. Budd was convinced that they were not the words his visitor had originally intended to say, but faced with the necessity of saying something in reply to the stout man's question he had said the first thing that came into his head.

'I think your lawyer is right,' he said. 'It wouldn't be much good your attemptin' to contest that will.'

Percy was quite obviously not very interested. His mind was fully occupied with the idea, whatever it was, that had suddenly come to him.

'You don't think so? I see,' he answered mechanically. 'Well, I'm very sorry to have troubled you. I just thought I'd like to get your advice, see? It's — it's — well, it's not a very pleasant prospect seeing all that money go to strangers.

'Very unfortunate for you,' said Mr. Budd politely.

'I suppose it can't be helped,' went on Percy rapidly. 'I'm sorry I bothered you.' He searched round for his hat, found it and twisted it uneasily in his fingers. 'I'll be getting along,' he said. 'Good night.'

He held out his hand nervously, and the big man gripped the limp fingers.

They were withdrawn almost instantly, but not before Mr. Budd had noticed the trembling of his hand.

He escorted Gottleib through the bar parlour, and saw him off the premises, returning to his room in a very thoughtful mood.

Just why had Percy come to see him?

The excuse he had made concerning the will was too thin to be taken seriously for a moment. He had come on business that was far more important, and then, for some reason or other, had suddenly changed his mind. He had changed his mind at the moment of Mr. Budd's entrance, and decided not to say whatever it was he had come to say.

And he had gone away in a state of suppressed excitement. That was obvious in the trembling hand and the hard glitter in the little eyes.

Mr. Budd went back to his room and resumed his position on the bed. He lit another cigar and began to try and fit the separate pieces of this extraordinary case together so that they would make a coherent whole. But he did not get very far. Nothing seemed to make sense. These pieces that were in his possession would not match up. There were other pieces that he had not got which had to be found before the puzzle fitted.

Was the visit of Percy Gottleib one of these?

Mr. Budd thought it might be. He spent a long time wondering what Percy's original reason could have been for coming to see him, but he found no explanation.

It was just another puzzle to which he could find no answer.

★ ★ ★

Police Constable Archer was feeling very tired. He had spent eight hours patrolling the grounds of Mr. Criller's house, and when his relief arrived at twelve o'clock that night, he welcomed him with thankfulness. Visions of the supper, flanked by a jug of foaming beer, which Mrs. Archer would have in readiness for him, had proved very distracting during the last hour of his duty. Now that the pleasant prospect of that meal was nearing fulfilment, he felt a glow of anticipation filling his big frame.

At the little white gate on which Mr. Criller had discovered the scrawled symbol which had been the prologue to the double tragedy that had followed, Archer bade good night to his fellow policeman, who was also looking forward to his home and a good meal, but who lived in the opposite direction, and set off along the lane to his cottage and his creature comforts.

The cottage was one of a small row that was sited on the outskirts of the village. The cottages were near the drive gates of the Gottleib's house, and his quickest way was a short cut through the wood in which Grace Hatton had so unpleasantly encountered Percy Gottleib on the day she had been rescued by the opportune arrival of Jim Longdon.

The night was dark and starless. Somewhere behind the clouds was a new crescent moon. It had appeared fitfully during the evening but was now completely obscured.

But the darkness worried Constable Archer not at all. He knew every inch of the way; had traversed it many hundreds of times, both in darkness and in light, and could almost have found his way blindfolded. He knew exactly where he would encounter a depression or a rising hillock, and moved forward at a measured pace, his thoughts entirely concerned with what awaited him at the end of his journey.

At the beginning of the little wood, he paused for a moment to light a cigarette. The flame of the match seemed very bright in contrast to the darkness all round. When the cigarette was alight and the match put out, the darkness appeared more intense than before.

Police Constable Archer continued happily on his way, inhaling the smoke of his cigarette and allowing it to dribble through his nostrils with the enjoyment of the habitual smoker who has long been denied his solace.

No thoughts of murder or sudden death marred the tranquillity of his thoughts. At the moment he was more interested in the prospect of changing his heavy boots for the ease and comfort of his slippers, and anticipating how good the cold beef and beer would taste; in mapping out the little gardening job with which he proposed to fill in two hours of his after breakfast leisure on the morrow.

And yet, had he but known it, tragedy, stark and horrible, lurked, waiting for him, in the gloomy depths of the wood through which he must pass to reach the fulfilment of his desires.

No wonder that the moon, frightened at the thing which grinned up at the night sky, hid her face. The trees were mute, fearing even to whisper of the horror that their gaunt branches overhung. The very night shrank into itself as it mercifully covered with a pall of darkness the dreadful thing that had once been a man, but was now a limp heap of lifeless flesh, lying in the blood which had once pulsed strongly through its veins.

Constable Archer proceeded on his way, surefooted. He had, by now, negotiated the best part of the wood, following the little winding footpath automatically. Another fifty yards and the closely growing trees on either side would begin to thin.

His measured tread sounded clearly in the stillness of the night. Clop, clop, clop, clop . . .

And then, with a muttered oath, he stumbled.

He stumbled because his advancing foot had encountered, not the hard ground he had expected, but something that was soft and unpleasant. He fell forward, and putting out his hands to save himself, felt them come in contact with a warm wetness that was sticky . . .

He uttered an exclamation of disgust and flung himself back on his haunches. With one of those sticky, wet hands he reached for the electric lamp that was fastened to his belt. Jerking it loose, he pressed the button. A ray of light, blindingly white in the darkness, focussed on the object that had tripped him up . . .

A huddled thing, dressed in a well-cut suit of Harris tweed, the light colour of which was splashed and mottled with red — the same red that glistened on the constable's hands and was repeated, an ugly streak, on the contorted white face . . .

'God Almighty!' breathed Police Constable Archer, and stared with bulging eyes at that face.

The face of Percy Gottleib, whose snarling lips were drawn back in a grin of fear and terror that made his pasty face even more repulsive in death than it had been in life.

★ ★ ★

Mr. Budd got up with difficulty and moved out of the circle of light cast by the powerful lamp held in the hand of Police Constable Archer. He looked round at Superintendent Hawkins.

'The shot must have killed him instantly,' he said, shaking his head. 'It hit him full in the chest an' passed out under the left shoulder blade. From the amount o' blood, I should say it damaged one of the larger vessels of the heart. The doctor will be able to tell us about that. Our main business is to see if the murderer left any traces behind 'im.'

Hawkins nodded.

'It's getting rather horrible, this business,' he said in a hushed voice. 'First Brinn, then Gottleib, and now this chap. How do all these people link up with the murderer? What's the motive behind these murders?'

Mr. Budd wondered that. His big face was very grave as he looked down at the limp thing that had once been Percy Gottleib. It seemed scarcely possible to believe that that lifeless heap of flesh had, only a few hours before, been a living, breathing, thinking man. And yet it had only been a short time since he had seen Percy leave the inn. What had happened in that short time? Whom had Percy met after he had left Mr. Budd?

Archer, after his appalling discovery in the wood, had hurried post-haste to the police station and informed Hawkins. The local superintendent had, luckily, not yet gone home. He had been working late on the preparations for the inquest on the following morning. Hawkins, on his way to the scene of this fresh crime, had called for Mr. Budd, and together they had accompanied Archer back to the spot where the body lay.

There was no doubt from the beginning that Percy Gottleib had been the victim of murder. A search of the vicinity had failed to reveal any sign of a weapon.

Before leaving the police station Hawkins had telephoned to Doctor Swinley, but the doctor was out on a case. He had left instructions with the housekeeper for Swinley to come to the wood as soon as he returned, with a few details concerning what had happened, and the housekeeper had promised to inform the doctor as soon as he got back.

With the aid of Archer's powerful lamp, Mr. Budd began a systematic search of the vicinity of the body. There were no signs that any struggle had taken place. The earth all round was very damp and capable of readily taking impressions. If there had been any they would have been plainly visible.

It was possible to trace Percy's footsteps back along the path he would have taken if he had been coming from the direction of his house, but at the point where he had been killed these traces stopped. They did not extend at all in the opposite direction, although there were others. The impression of a large, square-toed shoe, and the print of Archer's regulation boots.

Percy had been coming from his own house when he had met the person who had shot him. Had he arranged to meet this unknown person, or was he on his way elsewhere when the murderer had come upon him suddenly?

Mr. Budd was of the opinion that the meeting had been prearranged. There was a little clearing at this point and on the right of the path three oak trees grew together in the shape of a triangle. It was the most likely spot in the entire wood that anyone wishing to arrange a meeting place would choose. The triangular placing of the trees marked it beyond any possibility of mistake.

On the other hand, if there had been no prearranged meeting, where had Percy been going? The most likely answer to this question, was to Mr. Criller's house.

Mr. Budd made a mental note to call on that unpleasant old man as soon as he had completed his investigations in the wood, and find out if he had been expecting the weedy youth that night.

Both he and Hawkins made a diligent search, but the reward for their activities was precisely nothing. Not the vestige of a clue to the identity of the murderer had been left behind.

A rough tracing of the square-toed shoe impression was taken. The soles of these showed that they were practically new, and from the shape it seemed likely that half the inhabitants of the village would be in possession of similar footgear. It looked like a standard workman's shoe.

They had finished their fruitless examination and were discussing this latest addition to the murderous design that was being woven round them, when Archer drew their attention to a flickering light that was coming towards them along the twisting path. As it drew nearer they saw that it came from the oil lamp of a bicycle, and, a few seconds later, the breathless figure of Doctor Swinley jumped off an ancient bicycle. He leaned the machine against a convenient tree and hurried over to them.

'Got your message,' he panted. 'What's happened this time, eh?'

In a few words they informed him. Doctor Swinley made little clucking noises with his tongue against his teeth.

'Dear me,' he said. 'This is terrible. Really, you know, this *is* terrible! The third murder in a week! I always thought this place was a one-eyed hole in which nothing ever happened!'

He dropped on his knees beside the body and made a hurried examination, accompanying it with a series of little gasps and grunts.

His verdict confirmed Mr. Budd's previous one.

'The bullet went through the left side of the heart,' he said. 'Probably nicked the left ventricle. That would account for all the blood . . . Don't suppose he ever knew what killed him.' He rose to his feet and rubbed the mud off the knees of his trousers. 'This is really shocking — shocking! Who d'you think can be going about dealing out sudden death in this appalling fashion, eh?'

He turned his twinkling eyes from Mr. Budd to Hawkins and back again.

The stout man shook his head.

'I've no idea, doctor,' he answered. 'I may as well be candid and say that the whole thing beats me.'

'And me,' grunted the local superintendent. 'So far as I can see, there's no sense in it all.'

'D'you think it can be a maniac?' asked the doctor.

'It'd have to be a clever maniac to've shot Gottleib in that room,' remarked Mr. Budd. 'A very clever maniac, indeed.'

He drew Hawkins aside.

'I'm goin' to have a word with Criller,' he said. 'I want ter find out if he was expectin' a visit from Percy Gottleib tonight.'

Hawkins nodded.

'All right,' he said. 'I'll wait here until the stretcher arrives to take away the body.'

Mr. Budd left him talking to Doctor Swinley and set off for Mr. Criller's house.

His thoughts were a mixture of annoyance and bewilderment. He could not see a single ray of light in the whole perplexing tangle. The murderer of Percy Gottleib was a totally unexpected development. Instead of helping to clarify the puzzle it only made it worse. Why had the pasty-faced youth been marked down as a victim by the unknown killer? Had he been murdered because he was an integral part of the main motive, or was his death a side-line, rendered necessary by something he had found out?

The big man was inclined to favour this latter supposition. He remembered Percy's visit to see him and his peculiar behaviour. He had called with the intention of saying something which he had left unsaid. Something which he had suddenly decided to keep to himself. Was it this which had made his death necessary? Had he, by some means or other, found out the truth concerning this business?

It was possible. But why had he, after calling to see Mr. Budd, presumably with the object of passing his knowledge on, suddenly changed his mind?

Mr. Budd was still pondering on this, when he reached the little white gate to Mr. Criller's house.

He was half way up the gravel path, which its owner so grandiloquently called the drive, when a hoarse voice challenged him and a ray of light split the darkness and focussed him in its glare. Behind the light he could dimly see the bulky form of a uniformed policeman.

'It's all right,' he called, and apparently the vigilant guardian of Mr. Criller's safety recognised him, for the light went out and the man came towards him.

'You going to the 'ouse, sir?' he said. 'I think they're all in bed.'

'Then they'll have to get up again!' replied Mr. Budd cheerfully. He was passing on his way when a thought struck him. 'Has anyone been in or out while you've been here?' he asked. 'Any member of the household, I mean.'

The constable shook his head.

'No, sir,' he replied. 'I ain't seen anybody. The place was all in darkness when I come to relieve Archer, sir.'

190

Mr. Budd thanked him and continued on his way up the path.

The house was in complete darkness when he reached the porch. There was not a chink of light to be seen anywhere. Mr. Budd mounted the steps to the front door and pressed the bell.

He heard the shrill trill of it inside the silent house, but nobody came to answer his summons. After a moment or two, he rang again. He was about to ring for the third time when a light appeared behind the glass panels on either side of the door, and a woman's voice inquired, huskily: 'Who's there?'

'The police,' answered Mr. Budd shortly. 'I want to see Mr. Criller.'

He heard the rasp of drawing bolts and the rattle of a chain. The door opened.

Mr. Criller's housekeeper, arrayed in a grey woollen dressing gown, peered out at him.

'The master's been in bed for some time,' she said. 'I don't think he'll like being wakened. Is it important?'

'It's very important,' said Mr. Budd.

'I'm afraid he'll have to be wakened, whether he likes it or not. Tell him the matter is urgent an' that I want to see him at once.'

The housekeeper eyed him dubiously, and rather ungraciously invited him into the hall.

'If you'll wait here, I'll tell Mr. Criller,' she said.

She went slowly up the staircase. Presently, Mr. Budd could hear her knocking on a door above.

Mr. Criller evidently took a great deal of rousing, for the knocking was repeated several times before Mr. Budd heard the faint murmur of voices.

'What the devil does he want at this hour of the night?' The high-pitched voice of the old man suddenly rose in querulous annoyance. 'All right, all right, I'll come down. Why can't these people come at reasonable hours, eh?'

Mr. Criller appeared a minute or two later, a dressing gown draped round his skinny form, his brows drawn together in a frown of ill-temper.

'What is it?' he snarled as he saw Mr.

Budd. 'What do you want with me at this time of night?'

'I want a few words with you in private,' answered the big man. He emphasised the word 'private' as he saw the grey-haired housekeeper listening from the landing.

'Couldn't you have chosen some other time than the middle of the night?' grumbled the old man. He shuffled across to the door of the drawing room and opened it. 'Come in here.'

He ushered Mr. Budd into the big room and closed the door.

'Now what is it?' he snapped irritably. 'Hurry up, I want to go back to bed.'

Mr. Budd told him of the finding of Percy in the little wood.

'Why wake me up in the middle of the night to tell me that?' snarled the old man. 'If the young fool likes to get himself killed, it's no concern of mine, is it?'

'I'm not so sure of that,' retorted Mr. Budd, shocked at the other's callousness. 'It seems to me likely that young Gottleib was killed by the same person who murdered his foster-father an' Franklin

Brinn. If that's the case, it concerns you pretty closely.'

'You mean, it may be my turn next?' said Mr. Criller, a little more mildly. 'Well, there's something in that, I suppose. I don't expect those wooden-headed policemen, who are trampling about all over my grounds, would offer much protection. Why have you come to see me?'

'I want to know,' answered Mr. Budd, 'if you've seen anythin' of young Gottleib tonight?'

'Seen anything of him? No, why should I?' growled the old man, blinking at him. 'I couldn't stand the fellow and he hated the sight of me, so why should I be likely to see him?'

'It struck me he might have been on his way here, or returnin' from here, when he was killed,' explained Mr. Budd, stifling a yawn. 'Comin' from his house to yours, he would naturally walk through the wood.'

'I've seen nothing of him,' declared Mr. Criller, shaking his head. 'Nothing at all. Is that all you've dragged me out of bed to ask?'

'Mostly, but not entirely,' answered the stout man. 'Have you ever heard of George Hammond an' Cecil Purvis?'

He deliberately put the question abruptly and had the satisfaction of seeing a flicker of uneasiness flash for a second in the old man's faded eyes. It was only fleeting, but he noted it and registered the fact.

'Never heard of 'em,' answered Mr. Criller. 'Who are they?'

Mr. Budd was pretty sure that he was lying, but he gave no outward sign of this belief.

'They're the people who are goin' ter get Sir Benjamin Gottleib's fortune,' he answered, 'if they're still alive.'

An expression of startled surprise crossed the yellow face before him.

'Come into Gottleib's money, do they?' he grunted. 'Huh! How did you hear about it?'

Mr. Budd told him of the lawyer's visit.

'Queer,' commented the old man. 'Wonder why he left his money to these people? I always thought that pasty-faced adopted son of his would get it. No, I've never heard of either of 'em. Now, if you're satisfied, I'm going back to bed!'

Without waiting for a reply, he opened the door and walked out into the hall.

'You can let yourself out,' he called ungraciously, as he began to ascend the stairs, and as Mr. Budd opened the massive front door, he heard him shout to the housekeeper: 'After that man's gone, lock up!'

An unpleasant character, thought the stout superintendent, as he prepared to go back to Hawkins. Hard, selfish, and with more than the touch of the miser about him. The type who would do almost anything to acquire money. A bit of a liar, too. He had heard both those names before. That momentary expression in his eyes had given him away.

On his way to the gate, Mr. Budd met the constable again.

'You managed to wake them up, then, sir?' inquired the man, and he nodded.

'Yes,' he replied. 'Pretty monotonous job you've got, guardin' this place.'

The policeman shrugged his broad shoulders.

'No more so than ordinary police duty round these parts, sir,' he replied. 'It's not very excitin'. Nuthin' ever happens much, you know. Not like a town.'

Mr. Budd thought that this must be the understatement of the age. Nearly everything had been happening lately. He wished the constable good night and proceeded on his way.

The body of Percy Gobbleib had just been lifted on to a hand stretcher when he came to the little clearing in the wood. Hawkins saw him approaching and walked to meet him.

'Well, did you learn anything from Criller?' he asked.

Mr. Budd related the gist of his interview with the old man.

'H'm. Well, if he wasn't going or coming from Criller's what was he doing in the wood?' muttered the local superintendent.

'It seems likely that he came to keep an appointment with the murderer,' suggested Mr. Budd. 'That's a fairly sensible reason, isn't it?'

'Perhaps the servants at his home could

tell us something,' said Hawkins. 'Suppose we go along there now?'

Mr. Budd agreed to this suggestion, and Hawkins went over to give some final instructions to the stretcher bearers.

Doctor Swinley, who had been leaning against his bicycle, raised his head and announced his intention of going home.

'I can't do any more here,' he said. 'Of course, there will have to be an autopsy. I'll let you have a preliminary report in the morning.'

'Right you are, doctor,' said Hawkins. 'You carry on.'

The doctor climbed on his machine and pedalled away.

As soon as the remains of Percy Gottleib had started on their way to the ambulance, which had been left on the road near the entrance to the wood, Mr. Budd and Hawkins started for the dead man's house.

They were admitted by the sleepy-eyed butler, who was horrified to hear their news.

The murder of Percy, coming so soon after the death of Gottleib senior, created consternation among the servants, but none of them could offer any helpful information. The young man had spent the greater part of that evening in his foster-father's study going through a mass of papers. He had given orders that he was not to be disturbed, but had rung about nine o'clock for some whisky to be brought in. At ten o'clock, he had gone out without saying how long he would be, or where he was going, and that was all.

It had been a quarter to eleven when he had called to see Mr. Budd at the inn. He must have gone straight there after leaving the house. And while he had been speaking to Mr. Budd, a sudden thought had occurred to him and he stopped — almost in the middle of a sentence. Whatever he had really come to say had remained unsaid. Rather abruptly he had terminated the interview and gone — where? To the wood in which he had met with his death? Unless he had previously arranged an appointment there with the murderer. It seemed unlikely, for it lay entirely out of his way.

The stout man put a question to the

butler, and the man shook his head.

'So far as I know,' he replied, 'Mr. Percy had no intimate friends in the neighbourhood. Nearly all his friends lived in London.'

At Mr. Budd's request they were taken to the study, and with Hawkins's help he searched through the pile of untidy papers on the big desk.

Percy had apparently been going carefully through every document and paper in the house, presumably in the hope of finding some reference to the two mysterious men to whom his foster-father had willed his money. Had he discovered anything?

At the end of their examination, neither Mr. Budd nor superintendent Hawkins, had found anything that was of the least help. There was nothing with any reference to either of the people mentioned in that extraordinary will.

But had Percy Gottleib found anything?

Was it because he *had* found something that he had come post-haste to Mr. Budd?

It seemed quite likely. From the state of the desk it was obvious that he had gone out hurriedly. He hadn't waited to put the litter of papers away.

But if he had found something where was it?

There was only one answer to that.

He had had it with him at the time he had met his death and the murderer had taken it from him!

★ ★ ★

Jim Longdon came into the dining room five minutes late for breakfast, muttered an apologetic 'good-morning' to his mother, and took his place at the table.

His face was pale, and the dark, purple marks under his eyes testified to his restless and sleepless night.

The weather had changed and a cold, damp mist enveloped everything. Through it the shadowy trees dripped monotonously on to the carpet of fallen leaves.

It was depressing outside and some of the morning's melancholy atmosphere had drifted into the pleasant dining room, for the two people at the table were morose and silent.

Helen Longdon nibbled at a slice of dry toast and sipped a cup of coffee. Jim, although he helped himself to kidney's and bacon, and made a pretence of eating, there was very nearly as much on his plate when he had finished as when he had started.

His mother raised her eyes from her plate as he got up and went over to the fire, staring at his back speculatively.

'Are you still worrying?' she asked at last gently.

He swung round.

'Of course, I'm worrying,' he said. 'How can I help it? It was a mad thing to do! Supposing the police find out? What's going to happen then?'

She came over and joined him, taking up her favourite position with one elbow on the mantelpiece.

'They couldn't prove anything,' she answered after a pause.

'You can't be sure of that,' he said. 'Somebody may have seen you entering the drive . . . '

She shook her head.

'There was nobody about,' she interrupted. 'I was very careful to make sure . . . '

'All the same . . . ' he began, and stopped abruptly as there came a tap on the door and a maid entered.

'What is it?' asked Mrs. Longdon sharply.

'If you please, ma'am,' said the girl, 'it's the police. They want to see you.'

Jim uttered an exclamation and his mother shot him a warning glance.

'Where are they?' she asked.

'They're waiting in the hall, ma'am,' answered the girl.

'Show them into the drawing room,' said Mrs. Longdon evenly. 'I will come in a moment.'

The maid withdrew, closing the door, and Jim, his face suddenly white and strained, turned to his mother.

'So they *have* found out,' he whispered hoarsely. 'What are you . . . ?'

'Don't be silly,' she broke in impatiently. 'They've probably come about the robbery.'

The colour came back to his cheeks.

'Of course,' he said, and there was relief in his voice. 'I'd forgotten all about that. I expect you're right.'

Mrs. Longdon smiled and walked to the door. As her fingers closed on the handles, she turned and looked back. But if she had been going to say anything, she thought better of it, turned the handle firmly and went out.

The two men who were waiting in the drawing room, looked round from the window as she came in. Superintendent Hawkins she knew, but the big, sleepy-eyed man who was with him was a stranger to her.

'You wish to see me?' she asked quietly.

'Yes, madam,' answered Hawkins. 'I'm very sorry to disturb you, but I believe you may be able to give us some information.

'About the robbery?' she said. 'I think I gave you all the informa . . .'

'No, madam,' interrupted Hawkins, shaking his head, 'Not about the robbery. In connection with these murders.'

Not by so much as the flicker of an

eyelid did she betray the panic that came over her. They couldn't know! It was impossible!

'I'm afraid, I don't understand you,' she said calmly. 'How can *I* possibly help you?'

She faced them, a slight expression of puzzlement in her eyes.

Hawkins cleared his throat while he searched for a way to begin.

'Information has reached us, madam,' he said, 'which leads us to believe that you were acquainted with the two men who were killed.'

'Then I'm afraid that your information is inaccurate,' she retorted. 'I knew neither of them.'

The local superintendent coughed again and glanced at Mr. Budd. He was feeling a trifle uncomfortable. In the circumstances his position was an awkward one.

It had been the stout man's suggestion that they should pay this visit, and Hawkins had only agreed with reluctance. He had nothing to go on except the statement of a known crook which might be completely untrue. Men of Mr. Whipper's calibre were noted for their sensation loving proclivities. They would make any statement for the sake of a little limelight. There was no reason to suppose that the little burglar was any different, in fact they had evidence, in what he had accused the police, that he wasn't.

And the Longdons were friends of the Chief Constable's. Hawkins's position was understandable.

Mr. Budd saw his difficulty and came to the rescue. He had no awkward association to overcome. He was a stranger, carrying out his job to the best of his ability.

'We was given to understand, Mrs. Longdon,' he said, 'that Mr. Brinn and Sir Benjamin Gottleib were acquainted with your late husband.'

She had, until he spoke, been looking fixedly at Hawkins to that individual's obvious embarrassment. Now, at the sound of this slow, lethargic voice, she turned her head and transferred her gaze to Mr. Budd.

Hawkins hastened to introduce him.

She bowed to acknowledge the introduction but her face remained a blank mask.

'Is it permissible to inquire the source of your information?' she asked unmoved.

Mr. Budd shook his head slowly.

'I'm afraid that would be givin' away police secrets, ma'am,' he answered. 'The question is, is there any truth in it?'

She took a deep breath.

'There is no truth in it,' she declared definitely.

Hawkins looked relieved.

'Your husband, I understand, has been dead for some time?' continued the stout superintendent, pulling gently at the lobe of his left ear.

She inclined her head.

'How long?' he asked.

'More than twenty years,' she said in a low voice.

'And you are sure that 'e never knew these men?'

'Quite sure. I was acquainted with all my husband's friends.'

'These men may not actually have been friends,' persisted Mr. Budd.

She made no reply.

'Do you know Mr. Criller?' he went on.

'I know *of* him,' she answered. 'The same as I was, of course, aware of the existence of Sir Benjamin Gottleib, but that is all.'

'I'm sorry if my next question should be a painful one,' murmured Mr. Budd apologetically. 'How did your husband die, Mrs. Longdon?'

For the first time during that interview the stony mask slipped. It was only for a moment, but the stout man saw the spasm which contorted the white, rigid face of the woman before him.

'Why do you ask that?' she whispered. 'What has it to do with — with this business?'

'That's what I'm tryin' to find out, ma'am,' said Mr. Budd. 'You needn't answer any of these questions unless you like, Mrs. Longdon, but I would like to remind you that three murders have been committed, and it's everyone's duty to help the police as much as possible.'

The watchful Mr. Budd saw her face

change. A look of surprise came into her eyes.

'Three murders?' she repeated. 'But I thought . . . '

'Percy Gottleib was shot last night in the wood behind Mr. Criller's house,' he explained as she paused.

Helen Longdon passed the tip of her tongue over her suddenly dry lips.

'How — terrible,' she whispered, and shook her head. 'I'm sorry, but I can't help you. I knew none of these people.'

Mr. Budd looked at her gravely.

'Are you prepared to swear, ma'am,' he asked, 'that these three men, Criller, Brinn, and Gottleib, had nothin' to do with the death of your husband?'

Her face went a shade paler but its determination did not relax.

'I am prepared to swear nothing,' she said firmly. 'I refuse to discuss the matter any further.'

Mr. Budd looked at her steadily, and his broad shoulders rose in a slight shrug.

'Very well, Mrs. Longdon,' he said. 'You're within your rights, of course. I was hopin', however, that you'd prefer to discuss this matter privately instead of publicly on oath.'

'What do you mean?' she demanded quickly.

'That is what will happen if you're subpoena'd for the inquest,' he answered quietly.

She frowned.

'In that event,' she said, 'I should reply to any questions to the best of my ability. Until then I have nothing more to say.'

She went to the door and opened it. The gesture of dismissal was pointed, and they had no other course than to go.

'She knows something, right enough,' grunted Hawkins, as they walked down the drive. 'It looks as though there was some truth in what Whipper said.'

'I never doubted it,' replied Mr. Budd. 'There's some sort o' mystery surroundin' the death o' Longdon. If there wasn't, there's no reason why she shouldn't've answered my question.'

'It shouldn't be difficult to find out,' said Hawkins. 'If he was murdered, as that entry in the diary Whipper says he saw, seems to suggest, there must be a record of the crime.'

'Maybe Weaver'll be able to tell us somethin' about that,' said Mr. Budd hopefully.

Hawkins sighed. His face was gloomy.

'It's a real snorter,' he said wearily. 'We're still up against the killing of Gottleib. That was a sheer impossibility.'

'It can't be impossible, because it 'appened,' said Mr. Budd. 'We're lookin' at it the wrong way, somehow.'

'You know the facts as well as I do,' grunted the local superintendent. 'There's no getting away from them. No one could've entered or left that room without being seen by one of us. Yet somebody shot him and got away with the weapon.'

'It's a bit difficult to explain,' admitted Mr. Budd. 'But there's got to *be* an explanation, you know. Maybe, sooner or later, we'll hit on it.'

He left Hawkins to attend the inquest, there was no need for him to go since it was only going to be a very short proceeding, and made his own way to the inn. There was a bulky letter awaiting him there which had come by the second post.

It was from Weaver as he saw from the envelope.

Carrying it up to his room, he ripped it open. There were several sheets of a closely typed report and a covering letter.

The man I put on to inquire into the history of the Longdons has turned up some very curious facts. See enclosed report WLKI03780. Their name is not Longdon, it is Singleton. Regarding Seton I have succeeded in tracing this man and find that he died fifteen years ago in poverty, leaving a child who seems to have disappeared completely. See enclosed report LAB 769880. I have not yet completed reports on Criller, Brinn, and Gottleib . . .

Mr. Budd pursed his lips as he read the letter. So the Longdons name was really Singleton, and Seton was dead.

He pulled a chair up to the fire, lit one of his black cigars, sat down heavily and, spreading the typewritten reports on his broad knee, began to read . . .

★   ★   ★

The report concerning Seton was brief.

The man had once been fairly well-off, but gambling on the Stock Exchange had soon reduced the ample fortune which he had inherited from his father.

The last remnant of this — twenty thousand pounds — he had invested in the Argent Mining Corporation, floated by Gottleib, Brinn, and Criller. He had lost the lot, and the shock had killed his wife, who had just given birth to a daughter.

Seton had vowed vengeance against the three men whom he swore had robbed him. But the only active steps he had taken to carry out this threat, was consulting a solicitor.

Seton broke up. He began to drink heavily, sank lower and lower, and eventually died of starvation, and acute alcoholism, in a tenement house in Lambeth. What happened to the child was unknown.

Was she dead, too? thought Mr. Budd. If not where was she now?

Mr. Budd laid aside the report dealing with Seton. Up to a point Mr. Criller's story had been substantiated. There *had* been a man called Seton who *had* invested twenty thousand pounds in a company which he and Gottleib and Brinn had been associated with. He had a motive for killing Brinn and Gottleib and threatening Criller.

But he had been dead for fifteen years so he could be ruled out of the suspects.

But there was the daughter. What had happened to her? Where was she? It seemed unlikely that she could have anything to do with this business, but there was always the possibility.

He turned his attention to the report on the Longdons. This was much more lengthy, and as he read, his interest grew.

The man, whom Weaver had put on to make the inquiries concerning the Longdons, had succeeded in tracing their connection with a certain Harold Singleton, who had been concerned in the Warrington bank smash twenty years previously.

Singleton, in conjunction with three other men, Joseph Conn, Sidney Watts, and James Rowley, had started Warrington's Bank, a private concern, that for some years enjoyed an enviable reputation in the Midlands for solidity.

How erroneous this reputation was, became evident when the police were rung up by a frightened servant one evening, and, going round to Singleton's flat, made the discovery that he had committed suicide.

He was found sprawling across the dining room table, on which were the remains of a meal, a revolver clutched in his hand, and a bullet wound in his head. The blood from this had formed a little pool on the table's polished surface.

The servants had been sent out after preparing the dinner, and on their return had discovered the tragedy. Singleton's wife and young son were staying with friends, so that he had been completely alone in the flat at the time of his death.

The reason for his suicide was quickly discovered. An inspection into the affairs of the bank revealed the fact that, instead of being the flourishing concern it was supposed to be, it was practically without funds of any kind.

Two days after the death of the managing director, Warrington's Bank failed to open its doors at the usual time, and the trusting depositors found that the money they had so confidently entrusted to its care might as well have been put down the nearest drain.

The dead man's fellow directors were horrified. They swore that they had left the entire management of the bank's affairs to Singleton, and they had no inkling of the true state of the position.

Naturally there was a long official inquiry but nothing could be proved against them. The suicide of Singleton seemed to be a tacit admission of his guilt. For many years he had been systematically embezzling the assets of the bank, and, when he found that nothing could prevent his depredations being discovered, he had taken the only way out and shot himself.

This was the general theory which nearly everyone believed to be the truth. The exception was Singleton's wife, who steadfastly refused to admit the possibility of her husband's guilt. What he had done with all the money he had taken from the bank had never been discovered.

Shortly after the tragedy, Mrs. Singleton had inherited a large sum of money from an aged aunt, and reverting to her maiden name of Longdon, went abroad with her son.

There was a lot more, but this was the gist of the report, and it supplied Mr. Budd with much food for thought.

It didn't require a great stretch of imagination to substitute the names of Conn, Watts, and Rowley, for Brinn, Gottleib, and Criller, and a very little more to conclude that they had not been as innocent in the Warrington Bank smash as they had persuaded everyone to believe. It looked to the big man as though Singleton had probably been used as a cat's-paw.

Mr. Budd searched in his pocket for another cigar, lit it, and sitting back in his chair, stared through the acrid smoke at the ceiling.

Here, at last, was the first tangible sign of a motive.

If Helen Longdon — or Singleton to give her her real name — was aware that the three men associated with her dead husband in the Warrington Bank catastrophe were Criller, Brinn, and Gottleib, and if she were under the impression that they had been responsible for Singleton's suicide, it was quite possible that she had planned to avenge her husband's death.

He remembered the handkerchief he had picked up at the beginning of the little path to the summerhouse on the morning of Brinn's death. That had belonged to Jim Longdon, and, discounting Grace Hatton's suggestion as to how it had got there, supplied another pointer to the Longdons.

The scrawled 'S' on the table-top fitted, too. The first letter in the name of Singleton.

But there was still the mystery of how Gottleib's murder had been carried out. That had to be shown before anything could be done. There was, also, the meaning of Gottleib's extraordinary will and the murder of Percy to be explained.

There was still a great deal to be found

out, a lot of questions to be answered, a number of loose ends to be neatly tied, before he could even take the possibility of the Longdons' guilt for granted.

Mr. Budd shook his head wearily.

Still, the reports supplied a starting point from which to begin further investigation. They, at least, provided something to work on.

The stout superintendent finished his cigar, opened the window to let out the foul smoke and fumes from the cigars he had smoked, collected the scattered sheets of the reports, and, folding them neatly, put them in his pocket.

Hawkins should be told about this fresh information at once, and Mr. Budd decided to go down to the police station and tell him.

The local superintendent was talking to the Chief Constable about the result of the inquest when he arrived. Major Candy, spick and span, and more reminiscent of the parade ground than ever, greeted him with a nod.

'Morning!' he snapped hoarsely. 'How d'you do, eh? Just talking about this fresh crime. Bad, y'know, very bad.'

Mr. Budd agreed that it was extremely bad.

'We shall have to get a move on, eh?' went on the Chief Constable, frowning at his immaculately polished shoes. 'Find this feller, whoever he is, who's lurking about the place killing people, eh? Be a panic if we don't, y'know.'

Below the silver smoothness of his hair, his forehead was creased into a worried frown.

'I've just had some fresh information from the Yard, sir,' said Mr. Budd taking the bundle of reports from his pocket and laying them on the desk. 'That's what brought me along.'

Major Candy's steely-blue eyes regarded him hopefully.

'Eh, fresh information?' said he. 'That's good. What's it all about, eh?'

Mr. Budd handed him the shorter report. The Chief Constable glanced quickly at it and passed it on to Hawkins.

'Well, that disposes of Seton,' remarked the local superintendent when he had read it. '*He* can't be the feller we're after.'

'No,' replied Mr. Budd. 'I never really believed in that story, you know. It always sounded a bit phoney to me. Tell me what you think of that.'

Hawkins picked up the other report. As he read it, his face changed. When he came to the end he uttered a low whistle.

'My word, this is something,' he exclaimed. 'Read that, sir.'

He got up and handed the report to Major Candy.

'What's this?' muttered the Chief Constable. 'What's this? Singleton? Who the devil's Singleton, eh?'

'Read it, sir,' said Hawkins.

Major Candy ran his eyes quickly down the typed sheet and uttered a startled exclamation.

'Begad,' he ejaculated. 'This is astounding — astounding!'

They watched him in silence until he had finished reading.

'Extraordinary,' he muttered, glaring from one to the other. 'Absolutely extraordinary! It looks as if this feller, what's-his-name, Whippit . . . '

'Whipper, sir,' corrected Hawkins gently.

'Eh? Oh, yes, yes, Whipper,' said the Major. 'It looks as if he'd been speaking the truth, eh?'

'There doesn't seem to be much doubt about that, sir,' said Mr. Budd. 'What he saw in that book on Mrs. Longdon's dressing-table is explained by this report.'

'But — good heavens, the Longdons!' cried Major Candy shaking his head helplessly. 'I can't believe it! It's — it's incredible — absolutely incredible . . . '

The telephone outside in the charge room rang loudly and shrilly. They heard the desk sergeant lift the receiver and answer the summons.

'That's right,' he said, and then his voice rose excitedly. '*What*? 'Ere, 'ol' on, will yer?'

They heard him get down from his stool and then his footsteps thudding on the bare floor as he ran across to the door of the office.

'Will you come to the phone, Super?' he cried, thrusting his head through the partly open door.

'What's the trouble, sergeant?' demanded Hawkins. 'Who rang?'

'It's Archer,' replied the sergeant. ''E says that Mr. Criller's just been shot!'

9

When Hawkins had had a brief conversation with the constable over the telephone they found that it was not so serious as the desk sergeant's words had led them to expect.

Mr. Criller had certainly been shot *at*, but the bullet had done little damage beyond drilling a neat hole through the crown of his hat.

'I've promised to go up to the house at once,' said the local superintendent. 'Are you coming?'

He addressed his remark to Mr. Budd, and that worthy man nodded.

'And you, sir?' Hawkins turned to his superior.

Major Candy looked at his watch and shook his head.

'I'd like to,' he said, 'but I'm afraid I can't. Got a luncheon appointment, and I'm late already. Ring me this afternoon, will you?'

He hurried away, and Mr. Budd and Hawkins set off for Mr. Criller's house.

The old man was sitting in front of the fire in the drawing room, sipping coffee when they arrived, and he greeted them with an unpleasant smile.

'Come to lock the stable door now that the horse has been stolen, eh?' he snarled. 'Your police guards are a lot of good! I might be dead now for all the use they are!'

He went on in this strain for some time, but eventually they were able to get a coherent story out of him.

According to this, he had felt the need of exercise and fresh air, and had decided to take a walk in his garden. The day being damp and a little chilly, he had put on his hat and overcoat. He was passing along a path that was lined with laurel bushes when his hat had suddenly been whisked from his head and he had been startled to hear the sound of a sharp report from somewhere close by.

'Did you see anybody?' asked Mr. Budd, leaning back in his chair and closing his eyes.

'No,' growled the old man. 'I heard somebody, though, moving quickly among the bushes.'

'I 'eard the report, sir,' put in Archer, red-faced and a little flustered, 'an' I ran in the direction from which it come. I found Mr. Criller just pickin' up 'is hat.'

'Did you make a search of the vicinity?' asked Hawkins.

The constable nodded.

'Both me an' Carter, sir,' he said. ''E heard the shot, too. But we didn't find nobody.'

'Any traces?' asked Mr. Budd.

'No, sir,' replied Archer. 'I don't think 'e could've been in the shrubbery after all, sir. There's a little lane beside it — just be'ind it — an' it's my opinion that's where 'e was, an' not in the garden at all.'

Hawkins wrinkled his forehead.

'I wonder how he *knew* that you were going for this walk?' he said, looking at the glowering Mr. Criller. 'It's hardly likely that he would've been waiting about on the off chance, is it? Don't you think that's funny?'

'I don't think any of it's funny!' snapped the old man. 'There's nothing humorous in being shot, I can tell you! This person has threatened me, killed two of my friends, and it seems quite likely to me that he would have been watching for a suitable opportunity to carry out his threat.'

'Who *did* know you was goin' out?' asked Mr. Budd.

'Miss Hatton and my housekeeper,' answered Mr. Criller, 'and the other constable, what's-his-name? — Carter. He saw me come out the front door.'

'I'd like to go and look at the place where this happened,' said Hawkins. 'Show me, will you, Archer?'

The constable moved obediently over to the door, and Mr. Budd rose laboriously to his feet.

'What do you expect to find?' grunted the old man. 'Do you think the fellow's still there, waiting for you to catch him?'

Nobody made any reply to this sarcastic pleasantry, and leaving Mr. Criller to finish his coffee in peace, they went out into the hall.

At the foot of the staircase they met Grace Hatton.

The girl's face was white, and Mr. Budd thought, from the look of her, that she had not had a great deal of sleep lately. She acknowledged his greeting with a faint smile and went into the drawing-room.

They heard the querulous voice of the old man demanding to know why she had been so long, as they went out the front door.

'I don't know that it would have been such a great loss if that bullet had gone through 'is head instead of his hat!' murmured Mr. Budd, and Hawkins grinned.

They followed Archer along a narrow, twisting path that ran between a thick patch of evergreen and a wide bed of bush roses. Half way along this, the constable stopped and looked round.

'This is the place, sir,' he announced, as they came up with him. 'The shot came from over there, accordin' to Mr. Criller.'

He pointed to the thickest part of the belt of shrubbery, beyond which Mr.

Budd could see the gaunt trunks of a little copse of trees.

'Where were you when you heard the report?' he asked.

''Alfway down the path leadin' to the gate, sir,' answered Archer.

'An' Carter?'

'Round the other side o' the 'ouse. We both 'eard it, an' we reached Mr. Criller almost at the same time.'

'And then you searched the bushes?' inquired Hawkins.

'That's right, sir. Carter took Mr. Criller back to the house, 'e was a bit shaken like, an' then 'e came back here an' helped me.'

'And you found nothing?'

Archer shook his head.

'No, sir.'

Mr. Budd frowned and rubbed his chin.

'May as well have a look while we're here,' he said.

He forced his way through the laurels, followed by Hawkins.

The progress of the two policemen was clearly visible. Their feet had churned up the wet earth in all directions. If there had ever been any traces of the unknown shooter they had been obliterated.

The shrubbery ended abruptly at a barbed wire fence which cut off Mr. Criller's little property from a lane, that was little more than a beaten track at the edge of a fringe of woodland.

With considerable difficulty, Mr. Budd climbed this fence and looked back at the bushes. As he had expected, they shut off all sight of the path along which the old man had been moving when the shot had carried away his hat. The shooter, therefore, could not have been standing on the footpath when he had fired.

For one thing he would have been unable to see his target, and for another he would have had to shoot through a mass of thick leaves and branches with a very good chance of having the bullet deflected.

The stout superintendent's eyes strayed to the tall trees that grew so close to the dividing fence. From one of these the path would have been clearly visible, and the bullet would have passed over the tops of the bushes without any danger of possible deflection.

Was this where the shot had come from?

Had the shooter climbed one of the trees to get a clear view?

Mr. Budd went over to the most likely of these trees and examined the trunk and the ground beneath, but there were no visible traces. He tried several of the others with the same result. Hawkins helped him, but after a careful search they found nothing to reward their diligence.

'I still think that's where he fired from,' said Mr. Budd, when they had finished. 'I don't see how he could have shot at Criller, except by climbing one of those trees.'

The local man agreed.

'He must've been careful not to leave any marks,' he said. 'There's never a dull moment, is there? Something seems to be always happening.'

'Yes,' said Mr. Budd thoughtfully. 'Somethin' does, doesn't it?'

There was nothing more they could do

there, and they made their way back to the house.

On a table in the hall was the old man's hat, which Archer had put there. Mr. Budd picked it up and looked at it with interest.

The bullet had passed through the soft felt, and the position of the holes bore out his theory that the shooter had fired from a tree, for they showed that it had been travelling at an acute angle.

He put the hat down and picked up a pair of leather gloves that lay beside it.

'Are these Mr. Criller's?' he asked, and Archer, who was standing beside him, nodded.

'Yes, sir, he was wearin' them,' he answered.

Mr. Budd was still looking at the gloves when Grace came out of the drawing-room. As she was passing him, he looked round, dropping the gloves back on the table.

'You're a friend of Mr. Longdon's, aren't you?' he said, as she stopped.

Her eyes showed the surprise she felt at the sudden question.

'Yes,' she answered. 'I think I told you that before.'

'And a friend of Mrs. Longdon's?'

She nodded.

'Do you know that 'Longdon' is not their real name?' he asked.

She was either a very good actress, he thought, or she was genuinely surprised.

'Not their real name?' she repeated. 'No, I didn't know that. What is their name, then?'

'Singleton,' said Mr. Budd, and stopped as he heard a strangled gasp from behind him.

Mr. Criller had followed the girl silently out of the drawing room and was standing in the middle of the hall. His yellow face was distorted and he glared at Mr. Budd as though he had seen a ghost.

'What did you say,' he croaked. '*What* was that you said just now?'

'I said,' replied Mr. Budd slowly, 'that the Longdons real name is Singleton . . . '

'You're lying!' screamed the old man, clutching at the stair rail. 'You're lying! You're trying to put one over on me . . . '

'I'm doin' nothin' of the sort,' broke in

the stout superintendent. 'Mrs. Longdon is the widow of Harold Singleton, who committed suicide twenty years ago at the time of the Warrington Bank smash. Longdon is her maiden name . . . '

'Singleton!' The yellow face of the old man was a dirty grey and his skinny hands shook. 'My God, and they've been here all the time . . . '

His voice trailed away to an incoherent muttering. Turning, he groped his way up the stairs like a drunken man, mumbling and mouthing as he went.

There was a curious expression on Mr. Budd's face as he stared after him.

For the first time he was beginning to get a glimmer of the truth.

★　★　★

Mr. Criller did not appear at luncheon that day, but gave orders that a tray was to be sent up to his room. Grace was grateful for this respite from his company, for Mr. Budd's revelation had left her in a state of stunned surprise. Beneath this, too, was a feeling of acute uneasiness

— the same uneasiness that had been the cause of her sleepless nights intensified, now, a thousandfold.

The lurking suspicion that had tormented her mind ever since the finding of the handkerchief on the path by the summerhouse had grown to such proportions that it was almost a certainty. She was sure, too, that her suspicion was shared by the police.

A longing to see Jim, and warn him, took possession of her, and this became so strong as the afternoon wore on that, greatly daring, she went to the study with the intention of telephoning to him.

Her hand was on the handle of the door before she remembered that the police had sealed up the room and that it was impossible to get in. The only thing she could do was to go down to the village and phone from there.

She put on her hat and coat and slipped out of the house. There would be trouble if Mr. Criller came down and wanted her, but she had to risk that.

The constable, who had relieved Archer, met her on the way to the gate, and touched his helmet. The sight of him, which ought to have given her a sense of security from the menace that lurked so close at hand, had the opposite effect. This big, stolid man, pacing so slowly towards the house, was a concrete proof of the vigilance of the law.

If Jim were mixed up in this business, how could he hope to evade the relentless organisation which the constable stood for?

She reached the little post office in the High Street rather out of breath, for she had almost run in her anxiety, and nodding to the old man behind the counter, shut herself in the single telephone box that occupied one dark corner.

Giving the number she wanted, she waited.

It was some time before she was connected, but to her relief it was Jim who answered.

'It's Grace,' she said, in answer to his curt inquiry.

'I must see you at once. It's urgent. Can you meet me somewhere — now?'

'What's the matter?' he asked quickly.

'I can't tell you over the telephone,' she answered. 'Can't you come out — for a few minutes?'

He was silent for a moment.

'I'll meet you in three minutes,' he said. 'Walk slowly up towards the house.'

She hung up the receiver with a sigh of relief, and left the little shop.

It was a gloomy afternoon. The white mist of the morning, which had cleared at noon, was coming back and was rapidly increasing in thickness. The night would bring with it a dense fog.

She turned out of the High Street and began to walk up the gentle slope that led to the gates of the Longdons' house. She was barely fifty yards from the entrance when a figure loomed out of the thickening mist, and she recognised Jim.

She thought he looked pale and worried as he greeted her anxiously.

'What's the matter, Grace?' he greeted, taking both her hands. 'What do you want to see me about so urgently? It must have been something terribly important, or you wouldn't have rung up. You've never done so before . . . '

'It is important,' she answered and hesitated.

Now that he was with her she realised how difficult it was going to be to put what she had to say into words He saw her embarrassment and tried, clumsily, to give her time to recover.

'Shall we walk along Holly Lane?' he said. 'We're not likely to meet anyone there.'

She agreed, and taking her arm he led her across the road to the mouth of the narrow lane he had mentioned. They followed the rutted track for some time in silence, the girl racking her brains to think of an opening.

It was Jim who first broke the silence.

'Come on,' he said gently. 'What's the matter? Has Criller been more than usually objectionable?'

She shook her head.

'It's nothing to do with Mr. Criller,' she answered.

'Then what is it?' he asked.

'I'm worried about you,' she answered.

He stared down at her, but she resolutely kept her face averted.

'About me?' he said. 'Why?'

She took her rapidly waning courage in both hands.

'Why didn't you tell me your name isn't Longdon?' she asked.

She was still looking straight ahead and so she did not see the sudden change that came over his face, but she heard the little catch in his breath and felt the fingers on her arm tighten.

'Who told you my name isn't Longdon?' he muttered.

'I heard — from the police this morning,' she replied.

He stopped — stopped so abruptly that she was not prepared and stumbled.

'I'm sorry,' he apologised, tightening his hold on her arm and saving her from falling. 'What did the police say?'

She told him.

'That's true,' he said when she had finished. 'It's all true. My real name is Singleton. It was my mother's wish that we should drop the name of Singleton.' He paused. 'We've called ourselves

'Longdon' ever since I was a boy,' he went on presently, speaking nervously and jerkily. 'There was a tragedy . . . my father committed suicide . . . twenty years ago. He was responsible for the Warrington Bank smash. You wouldn't remember that . . . '

'How dreadful,' she said as he paused again.

'It *was* dreadful,' he replied. 'My mother never really recovered from the shock. I said my father committed suicide, and, according to the law, that is the truth. But morally he was — murdered!'

She was shocked by the vehemence in his voice.

'Murdered?' she repeated. 'How do you mean?'

'It's too long a story to tell you now,' he said with a gesture, 'but he killed himself because he was driven to it — because he was afraid to face the consequences of the trap into which Criller and his crook associates had decoyed him.'

Her eyes opened wide in her astonishment.

'Mr. Criller?' she whispered. 'What . . . ?'

'Yes, Criller,' he interrupted harshly. 'And Brinn and Gottleib. They didn't call themselves by those names then. They engineered the whole swindle, embezzled the trust money belonging to the bank, and faked the books to make it look as though my father had been responsible. They were damned clever. Nobody suspected them. They got all the sympathy that was going. The entire blame was laid on my father, and, of course, his suicide clinched matters. It was as good as signing a confession of his guilt.'

Into the girl's eyes came a look of horror.

'You've known — all the time — that Mr. Criller and Mr. Brinn and Sir Benjamin Gottleib were — were these other men?' she said huskily. 'The men who — who did this to your father?'

He shook his head.

'Not all the time,' he answered. 'Not until a few months ago. But for all these years my mother has been trying to find the men who were responsible for my father's death. She employed a firm of private detectives. They proved the connection.'

'So that's why you asked so many questions about Mr. Criller?' she said, and he nodded. 'Is that the reason you became friendly with me?'

'It was at first,' he admitted candidly. 'Afterwards . . . Well, you know how I feel towards you.'

'Then it was . . . it was you who . . . who . . . ?' Her face was white and her voice shook, but her mouth was so dry that she could not finish the sentence.

'Who what?' he asked, and read the answer in her frightened eyes. 'You mean — did I kill these men? Good God, no!'

Her eyes searched his face desperately. She was apparently satisfied with what she saw, for she gave a little sigh of relief.

'I was afraid,' she whispered. 'I've been afraid ever since your handkerchief was found on the path near the place where Mr. Brinn was killed.'

He started.

'My handkerchief?' His exclamation was a question.

She told him of Mr. Budd's discovery

of the handkerchief on the morning of the murder, and his face went a shade paler.

'I don't know how it could have got there,' he muttered. 'I've never been near that path . . . ' He broke off abruptly and looked away in case she should see the expression of fear and doubt that had suddenly come to his face. That fear had lurked in his heart ever since he had heard of the murders . . .

'You know that the police suspect you, don't you?' said the girl. 'They *must* suspect you. They know that your real name is Singleton, and they probably know the circumstances of your father's death. Once they connect Mr. Criller, and the other two, with those men who swindled your father, they'll say that was the motive.'

Jim bit his lip and she watched him anxiously.

'I suppose they will,' he admitted, and then: 'Why did you trouble, if you thought, as you apparently did, that I was guilty?'

She flushed to a dull red.

'I thought . . . I wanted . . . I — I . . . '

She stammered in her confusion. 'I wanted to give you time to . . . Well, I hoped you would be able to do something . . . '

'You mean you wanted to give me time to get away?' he said.

She nodded slowly.

'Even though you thought I was guilty?'

Her answering 'yes' was so low as to be almost inaudible.

'Why?' he asked gently.

She made no reply.

'Why did you do it?' he persisted.

Suddenly she turned to him.

'It was because I love you very dearly,' she said candidly.

His arms went round her.

'Why didn't you say so before?' he asked, his lips close to her hair. 'Why didn't you tell me?'

For a moment she rested in his arms and then she pushed him away.

'Because I have no right,' she said. 'I've no right now — but I had to tell you . . . '

'Why have you no right?' he demanded quickly.

'You know I love you . . . I've asked you

to marry me again and again . . . '

'I know,' she interrupted, 'and I told you I couldn't. I told you that it was impossible. It's *still* impossible.'

'But why?' he said. 'We love each other — why can't we marry?'

'Because . . . ' she stopped and was silent.

He repeated his question.

'Because,' she said at last, 'I am married already — to Mr. Criller!'

Jim was so staggered by her revelation that for several seconds he could only stare at her foolishly, too astonished to speak.

At last he found his voice.

'You — you're married to that old devil?' he gasped incredulously.

She nodded.

Now that she had confessed her secret she was quite calm and collected.

'He married me four years ago, when I was eighteen,' she said. 'I'm married in the sense that I have been through the ceremony before the registrar, that's all. It's a marriage in name only.'

'But . . . he's old enough to be your

grandfather!' cried Jim Longdon. 'Why did you do it? You couldn't have been in love with him . . . '

'There was no question of love on either side,' she answered. 'He wished it, and he has been, in some ways, very kind to me.'

'What reason did he give for wishing to marry you?' he asked.

'He didn't give any reason,' she replied. 'He just ordered me to, the same as he might order me to take down a letter or anything else he wished . . . '

'And you consented?' interrupted Jim incredulously.

'What else could I do?' she asked. 'If you'd lived in the same house with Mr. Criller as long as I have, you'd realise that it's no good arguing with him. Besides, I *did* owe him something. He took me from the slums and gave me a good education, clothed and fed me. I felt that I was under a certain obligation to him . . . '

'But not to the extent of marrying him,' he exclaimed. 'Why didn't you tell me this before?'

'Because he wished the marriage kept

secret,' she said. 'He told everybody that I was his niece, and wished that I should pass under that relationship.'

'He must be crazy,' declared Jim. 'What in the world did he marry you for?'

'I asked him that once,' she answered, 'and he said that I was useful and cheap, and as his wife I wouldn't be able to leave him.'

He saw the method in the old man's apparent eccentricity. He had forced the girl to marry him so as to ensure her constant service. As his adopted daughter she might marry someone else and leave him; as his secretary she might get another job; as his wife she was legally bound to him for life.

The utter selfishness of the scheme made him compress his lips with anger. For the moment he forgot everything else.

'He ought to be horsewhipped!' he cried. 'I've never heard of anything so disgraceful!'

She smiled faintly at his vehemence.

'I'm glad I told you,' she said, 'and I'm glad I told you — what I had no right to tell you. Now you must forget both.

'I'll forget the one but not the other,' he answered, and before she realised it she was in his arms, for a brief moment all her doubts and fears forgotten . . .

★   ★   ★

Mr. Budd was a very busy man for the rest of that day.

He left Hawkins at Mr. Criller's house and walked back to the inn alone. He was convinced that the theory on which his mind was occupied at that moment was the right one. It remained to be seen if all the facts in his possession fitted. He found that to a great extent they did.

By the time he reached his room, the skeleton of the imaginary edifice he was erecting was complete.

He had a wash, came downstairs and inquired for the nearest telephone. The inn possessed nothing so modern and he was referred to the post office.

He strolled down to the little shop in the High Street and succeeded in getting through, after some difficulty, to Scotland Yard.

For nearly fifteen minutes he talked to Sergeant Leek.

'When you've done that,' he concluded, 'you'd better come down 'ere. Don't fall asleep on the way, will you?'

Cutting short the melancholy Leek's protests, Mr. Budd left the post office and went back to the inn, and ensconced himself before the fire in the deserted bar-parlour. He smoked two of his black cigars and was aroused from a deep reverie by the arrival of tea and muffins. He consumed three cups of tea and four muffins, absent-mindedly, and resumed his interrupted thoughts.

It was nearly half past six when he got up, yawned, stretched himself, and going over to the window, looked out. The threatened fog had kept its promise and enveloped everything in a thick, white mist that was practically impenetrable.

Mr. Budd grunted.

Not a pleasant night to go out, particularly in a district that was unfamiliar, but it was essential for him to go. He went up to his room, collected his hat and overcoat, and braved the choking vapour.

It was impossible to see more than three yards, but he managed to grope his way along until he saw the dim, blue light of the police station, a sickly blur, through the fog.

The desk sergeant stared at him across the misty charge room, recognised him, and smiled a greeting.

'The Sooper ain't back yet, sir,' he said, 'but I'm expectin' him any minute. Nasty night, ain't it?'

Mr. Budd heartily agreed with him.

Hawkins came in a few minutes later and looked at the stout man in surprise.

'Hello,' he said. 'I didn't expect to see you. Been waiting long?'

'Not very long,' said Mr. Budd, and followed the superintendent into his office.

'What's the news?' asked Hawkins hanging up his hat and coat.

'I think I've got a line on this business at last,' remarked Mr. Budd. 'I'm not sure yet, but I believe I'm right. It's goin' to be a little difficult to prove, though, but we ought to be able to manage it between us.'

He pulled up a chair and for over an hour he talked. Hawkins looked more and more astonished as he proceeded.

'That's my gen'ral theory,' concluded Mr. Budd. 'It isn't complete. There's a lot o' blanks to fill in, an' that's what we've got to work on.'

The local superintendent nodded slowly.

'You may have hit the jackpot,' he said.

There was a tap on the door, and the desk sergeant entered. He laid a long, official-looking envelope on the desk in front of Mr. Budd.

'Just come,' he said briefly, and withdrew.

The big man picked up the envelope and slit it open with a broad thumb. There was a letter and an enclosure inside. He read both, pursing his lips as he did so.

'This is from Weaver,' he said, looking up. 'It's about Franklin Brinn. Very little seems to've been known about him, but they've traced a lawyer who handled some of his affairs. This man states that he has a will made by Brinn ten years ago.'

'That's when Gottleib made his,'

remarked Hawkins. 'Who benefits by Brinn's will?'

'One of the legatees is George Hammond,' answered Mr. Budd, looking at him queerly. The other is a man we've never 'eard of — James Levis. Everythin' that Brinn dies possessed of is to be equally divided between 'em.'

10

The lugubrious Sergeant Leek arrived at twelve-thirty on the following morning, bringing with him, among other things a copy of the late Franklin Brinn's will. Mr. Budd had telephoned asking him to do this from the police station immediately after the receipt of the news from Weaver.

Almost word for word the will was a duplicate of Gottleib's, a copy of which the police had obtained from his solicitor.

In the event of Brinn's death, his estate was to be equally divided between George Hammond and James Levis. If either beneficiary predeceased the other, the whole amount was to go to the remaining one.

'The question is, who are these people?' grunted Hawkins. 'There's another one now — James Levis. Who are these mysterious men that we've never seen, eh?'

'They're not so mysterious,' remarked Mr. Budd.

'Do you know who they are?' demanded Hawkins.

'I think I do,' answered the stout man. 'So ought you if you think for a moment.'

Hawkins frowned. After a moment he shook his head.

'I don't know what you're getting at,' he said.

'It doesn't matter,' said Mr. Budd. 'You'll know soon enough. It's only George Hammond that we're interested in.'

'By Gosh!' Hawkins jumped to his feet. 'You don't mean that Hammond is . . . ?'

Mr. Budd stopped him with a warning gesture.

'Not so loud,' he said. 'There are people in the other bar . . . '

'Sorry,' mumbled Hawkins in a lower tone. 'But was I right?'

'Yes,' said Mr. Budd.

The local superintendent had gone with him to meet Leek and they had all three come back to the inn with Mr. Budd.

Hawkins slowly finished his beer.

'It looks as if we were nearing the end,' he said.

'I think we are,' agreed Mr. Budd.

When the local man had gone, he turned to the melancholy Leek, who was sipping orange squash.

'Now,' he said, 'how did you get on?'

Leek produced a bundle of papers from his pocket and cleared his throat.

'I've got the records of the Warrington Bank business, 'ere,' he said. 'Includin' an account of the inquest on Singleton.'

He handed over some sheets of typed reports to Mr. Budd.

'I'll look at these later,' said the stout superintendent, glancing at them. 'Go on. What else?'

'I went round to the bank,' said Leek, 'an' saw the manager. 'E was a bit frosty at first, but I used me personality, an 'e thawed a bit.'

'I wonder he didn't melt away,' snarled Mr. Budd. 'Go on.'

'I got the information you wanted,' said the long-suffering sergeant, consulting a notebook. 'Current account, credit balance, one thousand five 'undred and seven pounds. Deposit account, nil. Five years ago there was over a 'undred thousand pounds in that account, but it was gradually transferred to current account and withdrawn. Most o' the cheques was made payable to a firm of brokers in the City . . . '

'I expected somethin' like that,' murmured Mr. Budd. He felt in his waistcoat pocket for one of his cigars, and bit off the end carefully. 'We'll have to go very delicately about this business — very delicately indeed . . . '

★ ★ ★

Mr. Criller put in an appearance for tea, his first appearance since the name of Singleton had sent him scuttling to his room like a frightened rat to its hole. His yellow face was tinged with grey and there were heavy bags under his faded eyes.

He drank his tea and nibbled at a slice of toast, maintaining an almost complete silence. Grace was in the act of pouring him out a second cup, when the housemaid announced that Mr. Budd wanted to see him.

'Well, why don't you show him in?' growled the old man, and muttered something uncomplimentary under his breath as he took the cup from the girl.

He looked up with a scowl as Mr. Budd came in.

'What do you want this time?' he asked ungraciously.

The big man ignored the insulting tone.

'I just dropped in to ask you one or two questions,' he said, and without waiting for an invitation dropped heavily into an easy chair facing the old man.

Mr. Criller's scowl deepened.

'Questions?' he snarled. 'Haven't you asked enough questions? If the police put as much energy into *doing* as they do in *asking*, they might be more successful in catching this murdering scoundrel who's loose in the district.'

'We're doin' our best,' said Mr. Budd soothingly, and received a disparaging grunt. 'We can't make bricks without straw, you know. We can only keep on trying to collect further information.'

'Well, you can't get any more from me,' snapped the old man. 'I've told you all I know.'

'Not quite,' remarked Mr. Budd pleasantly. 'You haven't told me your connection with Harold Singleton, have you?'

Mr. Criller's face flushed dully.

'I don't know what you're talking about,' he grunted.

'That's not quite right, is it?' said Mr. Budd. 'Weren't you, Brinn, Sir Benjamin Gottleib, an' Harold Singleton, the original founders of Warrington's Bank?'

The old man glared at him but remained silent.

'After the bank went smash and Singleton committed suicide,' continued the big man almost genially, 'you an' Brinn an' Gottleib changed your names, didn't you?'

'Well, supposing we did?' snapped Mr. Criller. 'What's that got to do with you? We weren't guilty of any fraud or criminal act. Singleton was the man who ruined us, and a lot of other people as well. It

258

wasn't good for business to be remembered with that fiasco, even though we were completely innocent. That's why we changed our names.'

'Quite understandable,' agreed Mr. Budd. 'Would you mind tellin' me what name you was known by then?'

'Sidney Watts,' snarled the old man. 'Anything else?'

'You are aware,' said Mr. Budd, 'that the wife an' son of Harold Singleton are livin' near you? Don't you think they might be responsible for what's happened?'

'Why should they?' growled the other.

'They might be under the impression that Singleton's death was caused by you and your associates,' explained Mr. Budd smoothly. 'Quite mistakenly, of course.'

Mr. Criller shot him a suspicious glance.

'Is that the police theory?' he asked.

Mr. Budd shrugged his shoulders.

'We're inquiring into the possibility,' he answered evasively. 'Don't you think that the 'S' scrawled on your gate, an' again on the table-top in front of the body of

Brinn, might link up with Singleton?'

'Why?' asked Mr. Criller.

'It's obvious, isn't it?' answered the big man.

'It's only conjecture on your part,' growled the old man. 'Have you any proof that these Singleton people are guilty?'

Mr. Budd shook his head.

'No,' he said, getting laboriously to his feet. 'Did you know that Franklin Brinn left a will?'

'I'm not interested,' snapped the old man.

'I thought you might be,' said Mr. Budd coolly. 'He left all his property to a feller named George Hammond an' another feller named James Levis.'

Mr. Criller snorted.

'I suppose he's entitled to leave his property to whom he liked,' he growled.

'I suppose so,' said Mr. Budd. 'Only it's rather peculiar that Gottleib should've made a similar will, an' mentioned this man Hammond, isn't it?'

'Is it?' retorted Mr. Criller impatiently. 'I can't see why you want to waste your time over other people's wills. It could be better employed . . . '

'Have *you* made a will?' inquired the stout man.

The old man's eyes narrowed and his thin lips curled back in a sneer.

'I have,' he snapped. 'Would you like to see it?'

Mr. Budd yawned.

'I don't need to,' he answered. 'I can tell you who benefits, I think.'

'Very clever of you,' growled the old man, but his eyes were wary. 'Who?'

'Cecil Purvis and — James Levis,' said Mr. Budd, and without waiting for a reply took his leave.

Outside the white gate leading to the lane, he met Leek.

'Well?' he greeted the sergeant. 'What luck did you have?'

'I found it,' answered Leek. 'You was right.'

'I usually am!' asserted Mr. Budd immodestly and with great satisfaction. 'In the circumstances, I don't see how I could very well be wrong!'

* * *

A sharp frost set in during the night, and when Mr. Budd looked out of his bedroom window on the following morning, he found the countryside covered with a white rime which glistened in the red rays of the winter sun.

There was a sharp crispness in the air which was very pleasant after the clammy dampness of the fog.

Mr. Budd drew in fresh, invigorating breaths as he leaned out of the window and surveyed the landscape. With any luck the end of this day would also see the end of the business which had worried him for so long.

His mind was fully occupied, as he washed and dressed, with his programme for the day. There was a lot to be done yet. Although he was certain in his own mind, he had no concrete evidence — not sufficient for a conviction. A clever counsel would tear what he had got to shreds and there must be no risk of that. The case must be watertight, without any possible loophole. And that was not going to be easy.

It was the finding of evidence that

would convince a jury that had proved too much for the police on more than one occasion. It is not sufficient to *know* that a person is guilty. It has to be *proved* up to the hilt, and it is not always possible to find this proof.

This affair was a case in point. It might quite easily fail through sheer lack of proof.

At the back of his mind, Mr. Budd had a plan which he hoped would overcome this difficulty.

When he had had breakfast, he left Leek at the inn and walked up to the Longdon's house. He was there for nearly two hours, and when he left and made his way to the police station there was a satisfied smile on his big face.

Hawkins was in his office and, shortly after Mr. Budd got there, the Chief Constable put in an appearance.

To the two of them the stout man outlined his plans for the rest of the day. Major Candy looked dubious.

'Very irregular,' he grunted.

'I'm quite aware of that, sir,' said Mr. Budd, 'but I assure you it's the only way.'

The Chief Constable argued and the stout superintendent argued and Hawkins interjected a word now and again.

Eventually Mr. Budd had his way.

In the early hours of the afternoon an official of the local council called at Mr. Criller's house with a buff form, which, he explained, it was necessary for every inmate of the house to fill in. He pointed out to Grace, who interviewed him, that this must be done in block letters for the sake of clearness. It was concerned with a special census that they were taking. He was apologetic but firm. The form must be filled up there and then. He waited in the hall while the document was completed.

Curiously enough he went to no other house in the district, nor did he go anywhere near the council offices. His destination, after leaving Mr. Criller's, was the police station where he handed the form over to Superintendent Hawkins. A few hours later, enclosed in an envelope with several other documents, it was delivered to Mr. Budd at the inn.

Darkness had fallen when the stout

superintendent presented himself at Mr. Criller's establishment and asked to see the owner.

The old man came out to him in the hall.

'You again?' he remarked sarcastically. 'Why don't you move in? I'll ask my housekeeper to fix up a room.'

'There's no need to trouble,' said Mr. Budd. 'I think this will be my last visit.'

The faded eyes, sunk in their folds of wrinkled skin, looked at him keenly.

'Does that mean that you've succeeded, or that you've given it up?' demanded the old man.

'It means that I've succeeded,' said Mr. Budd quietly. 'I know who killed Franklin Brinn and Sir Benjamin Gottleib, shot Percy Gottleib in the wood an' put a bullet through your hat. I also know why.'

Mr. Criller's thin lips curled sardonically.

'Congratulations!' he sneered. 'Have you arrested this person?'

Mr. Budd shook his head.

'Not yet,' he said. 'I want to have a talk with you first — alone.'

265

'More questions?' snapped the old man. 'Or are you going to tell me some fairy stories?'

'I'm goin' to tell you a story,' said Mr. Budd, 'but I don't think it would come under the heading of a fairy tale.' He took a key from his pocket. 'Let's go into your study,' he suggested. 'There's no reason why it should remain sealed any longer.'

'Well, that's something to be thankful for,' grunted Mr. Criller. 'I shall at least be able to get on with my work.'

He stood beside him while Mr. Budd broke the seals and turned the key in the lock. The room was stuffy and smelt of stale air.

Switching on the lights, Mr. Budd went across to the window and opened one of the oblong ventilators above, drew the heavy curtains, and turned round.

Mr. Criller had already seated himself in the chair behind the desk — the chair in which Gottleib had been sitting when the bullet crashed through his brain.

'Now,' said the old man, 'let's have this story of yours, and don't take too long about it. It's not very warm in here.'

Mr. Budd shut the door and came back, sitting down ponderously in a chair that faced the other.

'It won't take very long,' he said. 'It's the story of a plot conceived by a man on the verge of ruin to try an' save 'imself goin' over the edge.' He paused but the old man behind the desk remained silent. 'This man I'm talkin' about has called himself by several names,' he went on. 'but his real name is George Hammond. Hammond knew that in the event of certain circumstances a large sum of money would come into his hands, an' so 'e set to work to make these circumstances happen. The first circumstance in the achievement of his object was that Brinn and Gottleib should die. It was also necessary that they should die without the slightest suspicion attachin' to him.

'He knew of their association with the Warrington Bank smash an' the suicide of Harold Singleton, an' he decided to use this as a cloak — a cover up for himself. Had anything happened to Gottleib, Brinn would have been instantly suspicious of this man Hammond an' *vice versa.* They knew that he had already committed one murder — the shootin' of Harold Singleton. This time it had been done with their connivance an' approval in order to cover up their own guilt in the bank business. It was those three who 'ad embezzled the money from the bank and used Singleton as a scapegoat. Singleton had to die or he would have given the truth away. His death was made to look like suicide to add greater colour to his guilt. They got away with it.'

Mr. Budd paused again but there was still no sign from the old man. He remained silent, his eyes fixed on the man in front of him.

'Hammond used the 'S' sign so as to make Gottleib think that it was somethin' ter do with Singleton when Brinn was killed. He also used it on the warnin's that he sent — to *himself* as well as his associate. In their early association with this feller Hammond, Brinn 'ad been known as Cecil Purvis an' Gottleib had used the name of James Levis. After the Warrington bank affair they each agreed to make a will, each one leaving his money an' property to be equally divided between the other two. Gottleib left his to Cecil Purvis an' George Hammond, Purvis bein' Brinn's other name. Franklin Brinn left his to George Hammond an' James Levis, Levis's other name bein' Gottleib. Hammond left his to Cecil Purvis an' James Levis. Now, accordin' to these wills, Brinn, alias Purvis, bein' dead, an' Gottleib, alias James Levis, bein' also dead, both their fortunes go to — George Hammond.'

Grey-faced and rigid, Mr. Criller stared across the big desk unblinkingly at the stout superintendent. As Mr. Budd stopped talking, he passed his tongue over his dry lips, but said nothing.

'I don't think there's any need to continue this story,' Mr. Budd continued, 'except to say that in searchin' through his foster-father's papers, Percy Gottleib discovered the real identity of George Hammond. He came round to tell me, but just as he was about to, it struck 'im that his knowledge could be turned into real money. Hammond would be willing to pay heavily for him to keep quiet.

Hammond was the man who had killed Brinn an' Gottleib, an' also killed Percy in the wood to keep his mouth shut. Hammond was the man who fired that shot through your hat. Hammond is — you!'

'It's lies — all lies!' screamed the old man suddenly finding his voice. 'This is a story you've made up. You've no proof!'

'It's the truth, Criller, an' you know it,' said Mr. Budd wearily. 'Your real name is George Hammond. When you fired that shot through your hat you forgot that an automatic pistol blows back when it's fired and leaves a mark on the hand that fires it. You was wearin' gloves, but I found that mark between the thumb and forefinger of the right hand glove. That's when I knew . . . Don't move!' he added sharply, as the old man took one of his hands off the desk. 'My sergeant is coverin' you — 'e has been most o' the time . . . '

He raised his eyes to the ceiling, and Criller, following the direction of his glance, saw that the rose from which the flex hung supporting the pendant light

270

above the desk had shifted to one side, revealing a round hole which it had covered. Through this projected the muzzle of a revolver that pointed directly at Mr. Criller's forehead.

'That's how you did the impossible,' said Mr. Budd, 'and shot Gottleib in a locked room with both the windows and the door closely guarded.'

★ ★ ★

'I think that's all,' said Mr. Budd after a pause.

Mr. Criller gave a little strangled gasp.

'When . . . how did you find that?' he croaked.

'Yesterday afternoon,' replied the stout man. 'While I was talkin' to you, Sergeant Leek was smuggled into your bedroom. He found the loose board under the carpet and discovered that interestin' little gadget. As soon as I suspected that it was you who shot Gottleib, I deduced that there must be some sort of aperture in the ceiling. You was in your room, which is above here, when the shot was

271

fired. There could be only one place in a lath an' plaster ceiling where such a hole could exist — under the rose in the middle . . .'

The old man's face was devoid of all colour. His long, lean hands gripped the arms of the chair and his eyes seemed to have receded farther into his head.

'I never thought that anyone would ever suspect,' he muttered.

'You thought you was too clever,' said Mr. Budd sadly. 'They all do, it's one of the reasons they're caught. It was you who scrawled that 'S' on your gate, an' sent that warnin' to yourself an' to Gottleib. I can prove that. I've got a specimen of your writin' in block capitals — that feller from the council got it this afternoon — an' a comparison with them warnin' letters shows that they're identical. You made a lot o' money an' you lost it by reckless an' foolish speculation. You're on the verge of goin' bankrupt. That's why you tried this scheme . . .'

A sound came from the old man, a harsh, rattling sound that Mr. Budd realised in surprise was intended for a laugh.

'Well, you seem to know all about it,' he said. 'I doubt if you've got sufficient proof for a conviction . . .'

A spasm of agony twisted his face into a mask that was scarcely human. For a second he sat, his mouth open, staring foolishly, and then with a little grunting sob he collapsed across the desk.

Mr. Budd was at his side in a moment. He suspected a trick but he quickly saw that this was no trick.

Mr. Criller had evaded all necessity for an earthly trial. His heart had failed him and he had gone where proofs for a conviction are not needed.

★ ★ ★

'It was a very smart piece of work. Very smart indeed,' said Major Candy later.

'Thank you, sir,' said the gratified Mr. Budd, looking sleepier than ever.

'I don't quite see,' said the Chief Constable frowning in an effort to see clearer, 'how the woman who broke into

Gottleib's house on the night he was killed, fits in.'

'That was Mrs. Singleton,' explained Mr. Budd. 'I've had the whole story from her. She was looking for some proof among Gottleib's papers that he had been responsible for the Warrington business. She's been trying for years to clear her late 'usband's name. She tried to break into Criller's house on the night before Brinn was killed but the locks there proved too much for her. She dropped her son's handkerchief on that occasion . . . '

'So that's how it got there,' murmured Hawkins.

'It was a surprise to me to learn that that gal Hatton was Criller's wife,' put in Major Candy. 'Extraordinary thing.'

'It was a surprise to me,' admitted Mr. Budd. 'I guessed her identity as soon as I had read that report on Seton. Of course, she was his daughter — the little girl who disappeared an' couldn't be traced . . . '

'I suppose she'll marry Jim Singleton,' said Hawkins. 'I always thought there was an attraction in that direction.'

'She deserves somethin',' said Mr. Budd. 'Anyone spendin' most of their life with Criller ought to get some sort o' reward!'

'She gets two,' said the Chief Constable. 'She gets Gottleib's money, and Brinn's money, and what little money Criller possessed when he died.

'An' all that'll go into the Singleton fam'ly,' remarked Mr. Budd, 'when she marries Jim Singleton. I can't imagine anythin' that would've annoyed Criller more. All the money he schemed to get hold of goin' into the Singleton fam'ly.'

THE END

We do hope that you have enjoyed reading this large print book.

Did you know that all of our titles are available for purchase?

We publish a wide range of high quality large print books including:
Romances, Mysteries, Classics
General Fiction
Non Fiction and Westerns

Special interest titles available in large print are:
The Little Oxford Dictionary
Music Book, Song Book
Hymn Book, Service Book

Also available from us courtesy of Oxford University Press:
Young Readers' Dictionary
(large print edition)
Young Readers' Thesaurus
(large print edition)

For further information or a free brochure, please contact us at:
Ulverscroft Large Print Books Ltd.,
The Green, Bradgate Road, Anstey,
Leicester, LE7 7FU, England.
Tel: (00 44) **0116 236 4325**
Fax: (00 44) **0116 234 0205**

S.T.A.R. FLIGHT

E.C. Tubb

The Kaltich invaders are cruelly prolonging their Earthmen serfs' lives and denying them the secret of instantaneous space travel, so desperately needed by a barbaric, overpopulated Earth. While the Kaltichs strip Earth of its riches, the Secret Terran Armed Resistance movement, STAR, opposes them — but it's only their agent, Martin Preston, who can possibly steal the aliens' secrets. If he fails, billions of people will starve — with no place to go to except to their graves.

THE SILENT WORLD

John Russell Fearn

Around the world there was total silence from Pole to Pole. Seas crashed noiselessly on rocky shores, hurricanes shrieked mutely across the China Sea. People shouted and were not heard; alarms and bells rang and yet were mute. The dead wall of silence was everywhere — the most strident sound was unable to break through it. Scientists were unprepared for The Silence. There was something amiss with the laws which governed sound — but that was only the beginning . . .

DOUBLE ILLUSION

Philip E. High

Earth — four hundred years from now — a rotten society in which mankind is doomed to die out — and one seemingly average man with incredible I.Q. potential . . . An ultra-intelligent computer is built and used to govern humanity — and all corruption in the world is eradicated. Mother Machine decides what's best for her human children — and it is done. But the all-powerful computer is turning mankind into zombies. The world's only hope lies in one outlawed, not-so-average man . . .

A WOMAN TO DIE FOR

Steve Hayes

When hard-nosed PI Mitch Holliday loses his licence, he helps his partner, Lionel Banks, to pick up a missing girl named Lila Hendricks. But everything goes wrong; Mitch is drawn into a world of money, murder and double-cross. Seduced by social- ite Claire Dixon's wealth — murder is now the name of the game. The target is a wealthy businessman with few redeeming qualities. Would Mitch, tough and cynical as he is, kill for the promise of love and money?

MEET JIMMY STRANGE

Ernest Dudley

Jimmy Strange was a mysterious young man who'd turn up when he was least expected; wherever there was trouble, he'd appear from behind some dark corner. No one knew much about him, though he was always a gentleman. He was never short of money, but where it came from no one knew. He wasn't a crook — yet they did say he could break into a house with the best of them — but always in a good cause . . .

SIX STRANGE CASES

Rafe McGregor

Private investigator Titus Farrow is doomed by an encounter with the Chambers Scroll; Roderick Langham solves the mystery of the 'Demeter' from his armchair by the sea; a failed author goes in search of the barghest for inspiration; a missing person case turns even nastier than blackmail; Sweeney Todd meets his match . . . These stories make a gripping journey through 'The King in Yellow', 'Dracula', 'Sweeney Todd', and the noir fiction of the pulp era.